NINTH LIFE

NINTH LIFE

Elizabeth Ferrars

Chivers Press
Bath, England

•

G.K. Hall & Co.
Waterville, Maine USA

This Large Print edition is published by Chivers Press, England, and by G.K. Hall & Co., USA.

Published in 2001 in the U.K. by arrangement with the Author c/o David Higham.

Published in 2001 in the U.S. by arrangement with Harold Ober Associates, Inc.

U.K. Hardcover   ISBN 0-7540-4570-6   (Chivers Large Print)
U.K. Softcover   ISBN 0-7540-4571-4   (Camden Large Print)
U.S. Softcover   ISBN 0-7838-9493-7   (Nightingale Series Edition)

The text of this Large Print edition is unabridged.
Other aspects of the book may vary from the original edition.

Set in 16 pt. New Times Roman.

Printed in Great Britain on acid-free paper.

British Library Cataloguing in Publication Data available

Library of Congress Cataloging-in-Publication Data

Ferrars, Elizabeth, 1907–
        Ninth life / by Elizabeth Ferrars.
            p.   cm.
        ISBN 0-7838-9493-7 (lg. print : sc : alk. paper)
            1. West Country (England)—Fiction. 2. Sisters—Fiction.
        3. Large type books. I. Title.
        PR6003.R458 N56 2001
        823'.912—dc21   2001024385

CHAPTER ONE

Until the Friday came on which she was to be allowed to go home, Caroline Dyer had no idea of how ill she would feel when she left the hospital. Everything had gone so smoothly. It was just a week since they had whisked out her appendix after her dramatic collapse in the office. Only twenty-four hours later they had allowed her to sit up in a chair and they had taken out the clips on Wednesday. She was a fine healthy young woman, the young doctor had told her, with nothing to worry about.

Probably because she was not a young woman any more, had never thought of herself as excessively healthy, and only rarely and secretly as fine, his words had made her feel practically ready to go home, to go back to work on the spot. But when she saw herself fully dressed for the first time since her illness, she was shocked into recognising the unpleasant truth. That dough-like pale face in the mirror, which she had thought sufficiently blooming while she was trailing around the ward in a dressing-gown, talking to people who were far more ill than she was, really suggested that she was just about ready to slip away into her grave. Her hair was in dingy strings, her eyes were sunken and heavy, and rouge and lipstick hardly helped at all, but only made her

1

look revoltingly raddled. And then, when she had been taken downstairs in the lift and had to walk to where a taxi waited, the distance felt never-ending to her shaky legs.

Thinking of the journey ahead, all the way to Dexter Abbas in Dorset, where she was to spend her convalescence with her sister, she felt a shiver of panic. It would be so much easier now to go straight home to her flat in Ealing. She could be there in less than half an hour, and even though there would be no one to cook for her, no one to bring her breakfast in bed, as Fenella had promised that she would if Caroline came to stay with her, at least she would have no exhausting journey to face, and no strangers either, like Harry Lyddon, Fenella's possibly very difficult husband.

The thought of having to face the man at last, when he had deliberately avoided her for two years, was weighing heavily on Caroline's mind. For some time after the marriage she had seen nothing surprising in the fact that he and she somehow did not meet. It was like Fenella to get married without letting anyone know of it until weeks afterwards, to wring all the excitement that she could out of the secrecy of it, to keep her husband in hiding. But in the end Caroline had had to face the fact that too much time was passing, that even for Fenella it was odd. Caroline had assumed then that Harry Lyddon simply did not wish to meet her. And since, in the circumstances, it seemed unlikely that her welcome at Dexter Abbas would be particularly warm, how much better it would have been if she had had the strength of mind to refuse Fenella's unexpected invitation.

It had been on the Tuesday that she had come drifting vaguely into the hospital, almost as if she had lost herself in the great place, and she had looked at Caroline so uncertainly that she might easily have been looking for somebody else. Clearly she had intended to talk of something else, not merely of Caroline's symptoms, and of whether or not she had all the books she wanted, and of the problem of her convalescence. But either the courage to say what she wanted had failed Fenella, or Caroline's understanding had failed her, as, she was afraid, it often had, even when she had done her very best to meet the abrupt demands on her sympathy that her younger sister had a way of making. For how could one not fail Fenella when it was so impossible to discover what she really wanted, what would have satisfied her?

And it was so wearing to fail. It used up your strength for nothing. As Caroline climbed into the taxi, the temptation to tell the driver to take her to her flat, instead of to Waterloo, was almost overwhelming.

What she had forgotten, until she was comfortably settled in a corner seat in an almost empty compartment, was that a train is a wonderfully peaceful place compared with a hospital ward. There was no coming and going of doctors and nurses, of patients and visitors, no one tried to talk to her, no radio blared. She soon slipped into a comfortable doze, from which she woke presently to see Basingstoke slipping by, then damp fields and bare trees and hedges and a few primroses beginning to open on the railway embankments. Then she slept again, and when the train reached Rudbourne, the station nearest to Dexter Abbas, she realised that the last three hours were the most restful that she had spent for some time.

She discovered, indeed, when she got out of the train, that she was feeling much better than when she had started. Suddenly it seemed wonderful to be out in the normal world again. It was wonderful to see so many people who were able to go briskly about their own business without help, without worrying about themselves. The sharp spring breeze, blowing from the sea, smelt like health itself after the dead, disinfected air of the hospital. Standing there, a small, composed-looking woman of forty, wearing the blue tweed coat by which her brother-in-law was to recognise her, she was in almost as happy and bewildered a state of mind as someone who has arrived for a first, longed-for visit in the loveliest of foreign countries.

She wished she knew what sort of man to

4

look out for. Fenella, in her short visit to the hospital, had said nothing about Harry's appearance. She had told Caroline that he had been a journalist, working on a paper in the north, that he had given up his job soon after they married for some reason that she hadn't made clear, and that now the two of them were running a guesthouse together. But it should not be difficult, Caroline thought, to pick him out. Fenella had never been attracted except by men who were noticeably taller than she was herself, and she was by no means a short woman, and besides, they had always had a striking amount of good looks. So all that Caroline had to do now was to look out for a man who was tall and very good-looking. And such men don't come in dozens.

'Miss Dyer?'

She started. She had seen the man who had just addressed her coming towards her, but had not even wondered if he could be Harry Lyddon. He was not much taller than she was herself. He had a brown, leathery face above which his close-cut fair hair looked almost white. His nose was short and flat, his upper lip was long, his chin was lopsided. His eyes were rather prominent, of an uncommonly intense blue and set unusually wide apart. By no strain of the imagination could he have been thought good-looking.

Picking up her suitcase, he asked, 'Is this all your luggage?' Then, because of the uncertainty that he saw on her face, he smiled and said, 'Didn't she describe me? Stupid of her. All she had to do was say I look like a slightly over-size jockey—and not so very much over-size. Then you couldn't have gone wrong, could you?'

The smile showed large, very white, even teeth and gave a surprising charm to his face. Taking her arm, he steered her towards the exit, walking with a springy, hurrying movement, rather too fast for her in her present state.

'Odd how we've never managed to meet before,' he remarked.

Caroline shrugged her shoulders. She found that she had no wish to let him see just how much the same thought was on her mind too.

He went on, 'Whose fault has it been, yours or Fenella's?'

'I don't suppose it's been anyone's,' she said with reserve. 'It just somehow happened, as it does when people are busy.'

'Busy—ah yes.' His tone was dry. 'But wouldn't it be interesting to know which of us is supposed to be the unpresentable one? Though I know that, I suppose. I've heard such a lot about you. Not that I've believed half of what I was told. If I had, I shouldn't be here. I'd have managed to have business in London.'

She gave him an astonished look. 'Was it really as bad as that?'

6

'Did I say bad? The trouble abo~~u~~
that it was all so good. So very good t~~h~~
have turned into one of the ogre~~s~~
existence if I hadn't been sceptical by ~~n~~

'That doesn't sound very like Fenella,' said
Caroline. 'As a matter of fact, I rather imagine
she's hardly talked about me at all.' It was a
fairly safe guess, because Fenella rarely talked
about other people. She talked about the
problems they caused her and the feelings in
herself that they stirred up, but the people
themselves always seemed to remain shadowy
to her, not quite real and only indirectly
important. 'I shouldn't be surprised if you
don't know any more about me than I do
about you.'

'You don't know much about me? Ah, that's
good.' Harry flashed another smile at her.
'Then we start fair. The little man, you see, is
sensitive, and Fenella sometimes gets queer
ideas into her head.'

'If she has any queer ideas about you,'
Caroline said, 'I haven't heard them yet.'

'Yet.' As they started to cross the car-park
towards a new white car, he turned his
amazingly blue eyes on her for a moment. 'An
important little word. I mustn't forget it.'

'I've hardly seen Fenella since you got
married,' she reminded him. 'We haven't had
much time to talk.'

'You saw her on Tuesday, didn't you?'

Caroline was still feeling the impact of that

7

ent glance. It seemed to her that in spite of the smile that had gone with it, there had been nothing friendly in the look, that it had merely probed her swiftly and coldly for anything that there might have been behind her words.

'In a hospital ward,' she said, 'with I don't know how many people looking on and doing their best to hear everything we said, just to help pass the time. If she has any grievances against you, it wasn't the time to air them.'

'Oh, it wouldn't worry me much if she merely aired her grievances.' Opening the boot of the car, he thrust Caroline's suitcase in and slammed the lid down again with a neat yet oddly violent gesture.

Waiting for him to unlock the car, she thought uncomfortably that it sounded almost as if he had been trying to discover whether or not Fenella had in truth visited her on Tuesday, or had gone somewhere else, had seen someone else. Only he must have known that a visit to a hospital doesn't last very long. For all that Caroline could have told him, Fenella might have seen half a dozen other people on the same afternoon. So perhaps he was merely talking at random, not thinking much about what he was saying, because the thought of those two years embarrassed him and he was curious how Fenella had tried to explain them away.

All the same, Caroline found her spirits sinking back into the deepest homesickness for her own flat, for the undisturbing emptiness she could have counted on finding there. It consisted of only two rooms, a draughty little bathroom and a rather inconvenient kitchen on the top floor of a shabby Victorian house, but during the years that she had lived there it had gradually grown to fit her so well that it had become like an old coat that slips on over everything, protects everything, conceals everything. Not that she had much to conceal, except the way in which the personality that she wore all day at the office, a cool, sharp, sometimes slightly fierce personality, tended to come apart at the seams as soon as she closed her door behind her. And oh, the relief that it was to let that happen!

As she got into the car, she slumped very wearily in her seat.

Harry, reaching for the ignition, asked cheerfully, 'Feeling terrible?'

'Just very tired,' she said.

'We'll soon be home.' He started the car. 'Ever been in these parts before?'

'Sometimes we came to the coast near here when I was a child,' she answered. 'Fenella wouldn't remember it. She was only a baby.'

'Yet she seemed to have a sentiment for the place when we bought the house,' he said, 'as if she felt she had roots of a sort here.'

'Perhaps from hearing me talk about it,' Caroline said. 'She was only three when our mother died and I don't think we ever came here after that.'

'In my opinion it's one of the best parts of England, and Dexter Abbas is one of the most attractive villages in it.' He manoeuvred the car into the stream of traffic moving slowly along the narrow main street. 'We're very lucky, you'll see. The house is quite old, the sort that gives you a chance to grow some roots, if you want to. Nice things, roots, don't you think?—though the paying guests, so-called, do rather trample around on them at present. Still, the good people are only a temporary expedient, till my freelancing gets going. Fenella told you about that, I expect.'

Caroline shook her head. She was thinking that roots on Harry Lyddon were a most improbable appendage, quite as improbable as on Fenella, and that they would have a far harder time developing than he seemed to think.

'She didn't explain why you gave up journalism,' she said.

'Well, I'd had twelve years of being a crime reporter,' he told her. 'Isn't that enough for anyone?'

'That must have given you plenty to write about now.'

'Oh yes, it was what people call a full life, by which they so often seem to mean a nasty one.'

He turned the car out of the main street, where a signpost said that it was three miles to Dexter Abbas, and in a minute or two they were driving along a narrow road between hawthorn hedges. The hedges were just faintly misted over with the first fresh green of spring and there were celandines in the grass beneath them. The clear sky was growing hazy with the beginning of twilight.

The village was in a fold of the downs, the smooth grassy slopes of the hills rising up in gentle undulations from the back doors of the white thatched cottages. Caroline saw a duck pond, a pub or two, a small church standing among tall-growing yews, then there was a stretch of empty road, then a small garage with petrol pumps. Here Harry turned the car to the left, following a road that climbed to a steep-sided cutting through the chalk hills, then descended into a cup-shaped valley.

'Here we are,' Harry said, as he turned the car in between stone gateposts. 'The house. Ours. How do you like it?'

It was an old house of grey stone, red-roofed, with lattice windows, standing among beeches and chestnuts. Probably it had once been a farmhouse. It had that modest, rambling, ramshackle air. There were hundreds of daffodils breaking through the rough grass in front of it. It had deep roots of its own, whether or not its new owners would ever be able to grow any.

As the car stopped the front door opened and Fenella came running out.

It was always a surprise to Caroline, when

she met her sister, that somehow she always managed to look almost exactly the same as when they had last seen each other, however long ago this might have been. Fenella never looked any older. She stayed as slim. She always wore the same sort of untidily attractive clothes. She kept her fair hair cut in the same way, hanging thick and straight down each side of her thin, long face, a face that had a distinctly odd sort of beauty, because there was actually something rather horse-like about it, and to have a horse-face and be beautiful, when you are not a horse, is unusual. And she had never grown out of an air of bewildered diffidence, which helped to keep her looking about seventeen years old instead of twenty-seven, and which so very misleadingly covered her immense, quiet purposefulness.

That day she was wearing an old green corduroy skirt, a yellow shirt with the sleeves rolled up, small gold earrings, battered, very high-heeled shoes and a stained plastic apron. Her long, slim, useless-looking hands were red and wet, as if she had come straight from the kitchen without waiting to dry them.

'Oh, then you found each other,' she remarked in surprise, as if she had had no faith that this could happen. She never had much faith that anything would happen as planned. She was no good at carrying out any plan herself, so why should she expect it of other people?

She had opened the car door and Caroline was starting to get out when Harry stopped her. A lean brown hand and wrist came shooting out like the head of a snake from the sleeve of his tweed jacket to grasp her arm. He would not let her stir until she had answered the question that he had asked her.

'How do you like it, Caroline? Aren't we lucky?' It was as if he needed applause for their luck, to be assured that they were to be envied.

She was too tired to make any but the most obvious answer. 'It's lovely, Harry. Of course you're lucky.'

'But you think we're fools to have come here, don't you? You can't see us making it work. You think we ought to have stayed up north in all that soot and filth and that I ought to have gone on nosing out all the beastly little assaults and swindles that are supposed to be news, though they're all exactly like one another, for the rest of my days. Say it—go on—you think we're fools.'

'I don't know whom you're arguing with, Harry. It doesn't sound like me,' she said.

'But you don't think we're lucky, do you?'

'Oh, Harry,' Fenella said protestingly, 'please don't start talking. Can't you see Caroline's utterly worn out. Caroline, you're going straight to bed, then I'll bring you some tea. Everything's ready for you.'

'Lucky Caroline.' Harry got out of the car

and went to fetch her suitcase from the boot. Exhausted as she was herself, she recognised the extraordinary vitality in his light, impatient walk, in all his quick gestures. 'Lucky to have such a good, kind sister to come to in such a nice house in the country, isn't she?'

Fenella frowned. 'Don't listen to him,' she said as she and Caroline followed him indoors. 'I think he's got into one of his funny moods. If you take any notice of him he sometimes goes on and on till he ends up telling you how awful everything is and how he's never had any luck all his life. Of course he doesn't mean it.'

Thinking that she would not like to have to swear to what Harry Lyddon meant about anything, Caroline followed Fenella up a steep, narrow staircase and along a passage which meandered from one low doorway to another with the crookedness of a stream finding its way between boulders. It had a beamed ceiling and an uneven floor. There was no sign of Harry, but one of the doors stood open and the suitcase was in the room inside.

CHAPTER TWO

They went in. The room had a low ceiling, white walls, a grey carpet and bright red curtains at the windows. They were small

14

casement windows, set deep in the thick walls, and they looked straight over the empty downland. A wood fire burned behind the curved bars of the fireplace. There were books, a radio, and a bowl of primroses on the table by the bed.

With a sigh of pleasure, Caroline sank on to the edge of the bed and felt its springs yield with a far kindlier welcome than that of her bed in the hospital.

'This is wonderful,' she said. 'I *am* lucky to have such a good, kind sister. You can tell Harry so from me—whatever he was really talking about.'

Fenella had remained in the doorway. She was looking round, checking up that everything had been done that ought to have been done to welcome a guest. She was always anxious to make the appropriate gesture. It was her way of propitiating all that she did not understand in other people.

'There's a hot-water bottle in the bed,' she said, 'and there are plenty of hangers in the cupboard, and the water's hot, if you want a bath. The bathroom's just opposite. And I'll bring you some tea, unless you'd prefer some sherry. I should think you'd probably prefer sherry, wouldn't you? We'll be having dinner in about an hour.'

Leaning back on the comfortable bed, Caroline said that she'd certainly prefer sherry.

'We're having *Wiener Schnitzel* and lemon

meringue pie,' Fenella went on. 'I hope that's all right for you.'

Caroline's heart sank abruptly. She was still inclined to think that a boiled egg was a heavy meal. But she managed to answer, 'It sounds perfect.'

'Did I tell you Harry does most of the cooking?' Fenella said. 'I do things like peeling potatoes and grating cheese and we've two women from the village who come in in the mornings and do most of the cleaning, but Harry does all the difficult things.'

'You aren't going to a lot of trouble just for me, are you?' Caroline said. 'You really mustn't.'

'Oh, it isn't any trouble,' said Fenella. 'Harry loves doing it. Besides, we have to feed the others.'

Somehow Caroline had forgotten about the others.

'I didn't realise you'd kept open through the winter,' she said. 'I shouldn't have thought it would pay.'

'I'm not quite sure that it does,' Fenella said. 'We've only two people staying, and that's meant we've had to keep the heating and the cleaning and so on going, just as if we were full up. But Harry said we couldn't afford to refuse them. I don't know. We did awfully well in the summer. We're close enough to the sea to keep busy from Easter till October. So I thought we'd shut down in the winter and

16

Harry could get ahead with some writing. But he said Mrs. Dewhurst and Mr. Sherwin turning up was a bit of luck for us. Anyway, they're both quite nice and give awfully little trouble. You'll meet them tomorrow, if you feel like getting up. You won't mind them.'

She came further into the room, sat down on the edge of the bed beside Caroline and tentatively reached for one of her hands.

'Caroline, I've been thinking about you far more than I expect you believe, even though I haven't written,' she said, and as if she were afraid that Caroline might snatch her hand away, suddenly closed her fingers on it tightly. 'You know I almost never write letters. I keep putting them off and then after a time I feel so bad about it, I simply *can't* write.'

'I know how it is,' Caroline said.

'And anyway, I can never think of anything to say. But I'm so glad you weren't too angry with me to come. I wanted you so badly.'

'Well, here I am.' Caroline heard herself using the tone of voice that she would have used if they had been meeting regularly every week or so.

'I hope you'll like it here and I hope you'll get well quickly and I hope you'll like Harry.'

'Of course I shall.'

'He has those funny moods sometimes, when he seems just to be trying to find a way of getting one worked up about nothing, but he's—he's—' Fenella hesitated, hunting for a

17

word to express some very profound bewilderment. 'He's really a *kind* person—at least, I think he is—in spite of the things he says. I generally try not to take much notice of what he says.'

'That sounds a bit hard on him.'

Fenella wrinkled her forehead. 'Of course, you always said I didn't know anything about what went on in other people, didn't you?' she said.

'Did I?' said Caroline. 'How disgustingly smug.'

'Oh, you always thought me a complete fool. Besides a lot of worse things.'

'I didn't, you know, but you always put the words in my mouth, just as you're doing now. Anyway, who does know what goes on inside other people? I certainly never have.'

'Harry does.' Fenella stood up and went to the door. 'Or he thinks he does. Or he pretends he thinks he does. He's—sort of subtle, I suppose the word is. Now you'd like that sherry, wouldn't you?'

'Just a minute, Fenella,' Caroline said. 'There's something I'd better ask you at once. I ought to have asked it the other day, when you came to see me, but somehow I forgot. It's how much you charge here?'

'Charge?' Fenella said blankly.

'Just so that I know what I'm in for, before I get too corrupted by luxury.' It was really to make it clear that she was not expecting

Fenella and Harry to keep her in their guesthouse for nothing.

Fenella laughed. 'But I never even thought . . . I mean, you're family. For heaven's sake, we aren't expecting you to *pay* us!'

'Please,' Caroline said. 'After all, it's how you make your living.'

'We don't need to make it out of you.'

'But—'

'No!' Fenella's voice suddenly went shrill. 'You're not to pay us. You're not to think of it. We don't need it. We've plenty of money. We—we've *too much* . . .' Her hand went to her mouth. Holding it there, as if in a panic to keep back words that were trying to pour out of her, she drew a deep breath and at the same time snatched a glance through the open door, up and down the passage. Then she gave an uneasy laugh. 'Harry'll never get down to any writing till we've no money left, so we're better off without it, we really are. Now get into bed. I'll bring that drink up in a few minutes.'

Caroline did as she was told. The bed was as comfortable as she had thought—and it felt wonderful to give up the struggle with her own weakness and relax in its warmth. Drowsiness fogged her brain almost immediately. She was almost asleep by the time that Fenella returned with a glass of sherry and it felt a tiresome effort to rouse herself to drink it. Presently it was even more of an effort to eat the dinner that Fenella brought up on a tray.

19

In fact, Caroline ate very little, although she recognised with interest that Harry's cooking was something special. It would be several days, however, before she was able to do it justice.

Afterwards Fenella came to sit with her for a while. She brought some knitting and worked at it spasmodically while they talked. Caroline found it an intriguing sight to watch. She had never known Fenella, in the past, object to sitting with her hands idle. She had immense energy when she cared to use it, but this kind of domestic activity was new. Very new, to judge by the frowning, the muttered counting, the exasperated fumbling and tugging at the wool that went with it.

She started to ask Caroline how things were going in the advertising office where she worked, and where Fenella herself had once worked for three unhappy months, but broke off to exclaim, 'Damn it, why didn't anyone ever teach me to do this kind of thing properly? I'm such a fool at all the really useful things.'

'If I'd tried to teach you, it would have been a case of the blind leading the blind,' said Caroline. 'And when it came to things like mending fuses and putting screws in straight, you were always much cleverer than I was.'

'Ah, but you were clever at other things, so it didn't matter.'

'For instance?'

20

Fenella put her head on one side, considering, but seemed unable to think of anything at which she was sure Caroline was clever.

'Well, never mind.' The knitting needles were clicking rhythmically for the moment. 'What are you doing these days?'

'I'm assistant to an assistant manager—Mr. Willis—new since your time.'

'Is that promotion?'

'It's better pay, anyway.'

'Time too, considering how long you've slaved for them. What do you actually have to do?'

'Well, I suppose my real job is trying to put myself between Mr. Willis's very sensitive ego and all the other sensitive egos in the office in time to stop blood being spilled.'

Fenella gave a bewildered shake of her head. 'I don't know how you can bear it. Everyone with a knife at someone else's back. That's how it always struck me. But you quite enjoy that, don't you?'

'Until my own ego gets a more than usually brutal battering. Then I decide—say two or three times a week—that I'll give in my notice tomorrow.'

'But you do enjoy a fight, you know you do.'

'Well, at the moment, it's true, I can't think of anything I want more than to get back into the battle, but usually I hate that side of it.'

'I don't understand it, how you can stick it,'

21

Fenella said with a sigh. 'They're such terrible people.'

'Oh no.'

'Terrible, ruthless people.'

'Not at all,' Caroline said positively, defending her friends. 'Or not most of them. They were wonderfully nice to me when I was ill. They sent me flowers—people I hardly knew—they came to see me, they told me to take as much time off as I wanted. And at the same time they said they didn't know how to get on without me, which was what I really wanted to be told.'

'One doesn't *have* to be ruthless, does one?' Frowning again at her knitting, which she had let sink on to her lap, Fenella was following her own line of thought. 'I don't believe it. One doesn't always have to think the worst of people. One doesn't always have to look for horrors under the surface.'

The intensity in her voice told Caroline that it was no longer the people in the office of whom she was thinking, but someone much nearer home.

The funny thing about it was that Caroline had always thought Fenella herself as ruthless as anyone she knew. Quietly, without explanations, covering up how determined she was on some course of action by that apparent vagueness of hers, Fenella had always gone her own way. If it hadn't been a way that had ever seemed to be leading anywhere, that had been

22

her own affair. She had always made that clear. Advice of any kind she had always regarded as a kind of criticism, to be rejected with careless, bitter words.

Remembering this, Caroline did not answer. She had made up her mind before coming to Dexter Abbas that she would say nothing, nothing whatever, that could possibly be taken for criticism. She had found in recent times that she had a great longing at last to be friends with her sister, even if this was a relationship that they had never yet successfully achieved. There had been too big a difference in their ages. As soon as Fenella had been old enough to think about it, she had resented Caroline's authority too much and Caroline had been too young to know how to exercise it tactfully. Also, Fenella had been jealous of the reliance that their father, a sick and discouraged man, retiring early from his work in the British Museum, had placed on the elder daughter, while Caroline had often been jealous of his far more demonstrative love for the younger one. But oughtn't it to be possible by now to put these things behind them?

Well, only if she were very, very careful, Caroline acknowledged to herself as she lay gazing drowsily up at the low ceiling on which the warm firelight flickered. Very, very careful of what she said, and she had never been much good at that. For years she had almost deliberately cultivated an aggressive manner of speech, because inside she was such a lost and shrinking person. She and Fenella were really surprisingly alike, she thought, only it happened that each had the habit of showing to the world the part of herself that the other kept hidden, and of hiding what the other showed.

The lengthening silence made Fenella say, 'You're awfully tired, aren't you? I'll leave you in peace.'

'No, don't go yet,' Caroline answered. 'Tell me some more about Harry.'

'What do you want to know about him?'

'Oh, everything. How did you meet him?'

'Oh, we just met. How *does* one meet people?'

'Can't you remember?'

'The very first time, you mean? But I didn't know then it would be anything important.'

'I should have thought meeting Harry for the first time would generally be a fairly electrifying experience.'

'Why?' Fenella asked quickly, defensively, as if she had detected a possible criticism already.

'Well, he's got a very—' Caroline fumbled for a word. 'A very strong personality. A very vivid one.'

'I know what you mean,' Fenella said, but rather distantly, as if Caroline were not hitting the right note. 'There's a sort of—of recklessness about him that strikes people like that. I've seen him do some quite extraordinary, crazy things without stopping to think for a moment. And I always get so angry about it. As a matter of fact, the first time we met . . .' She stopped, glaring at her knitting as if it had just done some mad reckless thing in her incompetent hands.

Caroline waited.

'We were each driving a car,' Fenella went on. 'It was in a village near Leeds. He was just in front of me and he stopped so suddenly, I rammed the back of his car. It didn't do it much damage, but my radiator just crumpled. I jumped out to swear at him, but before I even got started he'd jumped out too and gone running off as fast as he could towards a bridge over a horrid dirty little river and dived straight in.'

'Good heavens, just because you were swearing at him?'

'Of course not. He'd seen a child fall in. But the river was quite shallow and he could easily have cracked his skull, and for all he knew, the brat could swim.'

'And could it?'

'He never gave it a chance to show.'

'Well, brave, wasn't it, even if it was crazy?'

'Oh, of course.'

'And what did you do?'

'When he came out? I told him what I thought of his smashing my radiator.'

'And what did he do?'

25

'He drove me home. And after that we started meeting from time to time.'

'Where were you living then?'

'In Leeds.'

'Was it when you were secretary to that novelist?'

There was a pause, then Fenella started counting stitches. '. . . three, four, make one, knit two together . . . Yes, that's when it was, but why the hell did you have to say just that? It's the sort of thing you always say. You can't accept the fact that what I do simply isn't your business.'

Flustered, Caroline protested, 'I only asked—'

'Yes, of course, you only asked an innocent question! But even you aren't as innocent as to believe . . . Oh damn, I'm sorry, I didn't mean to pick a quarrel. I'm sorry, I'm sorry!' Getting up quickly, Fenella stooped over the bed to kiss Caroline's forehead. 'Don't take any notice of me. I'm glad you're here. I wanted to ask you ages ago. I want you to enjoy being here. Sleep well now.' She went to the door. 'Shall I turn the light out?'

'Yes, please,' Caroline said. 'I'm sorry I asked—'

'Never mind. Good night.'

'Good night, Fenella.'

The light went out and the door closed gently.

Punching up her pillow and turning on to

her side, Caroline admitted to herself that perhaps her question hadn't been as innocent as it had felt when she had heedlessly asked it, for of course she wasn't so innocent as to believe that Fenella had only been a secretary to that novelist. No one could be in such desperate need of a secretary as to employ Fenella for her shorthand and typing for more than a very short time, and she had stayed with him for more than a year. Or had said she had. The truth was that Caroline knew very little of her sister's life during the last five years.

She wondered how much Harry knew about it. Had it perhaps been partly a fear of what Caroline might inadvertently let drop, out of her very incomplete knowledge of Fenella's past, that had kept Fenella away, had made her keep Harry away for the two years since their marriage? Was Harry a very jealous man?

Resolving to be even more careful of everything she said than she had thought would be necessary, to guard her tongue as if it were a dangerous animal which must not at any cost be let loose to ravage the peace and happiness of her sister's life, Caroline shut her eyes and settled down to sleep.

But now she could not sleep at all. There was deep silence round the house. The only sounds were the occasional barking of a dog, the crowing of a cock, mistakenly welcoming an imaginary dawn, and a metallic sound of hammering in the distance. None of the sounds was loud, but they all came at irregular intervals, and disturbed her far more than the steady hum of traffic, to which she was accustomed.

Besides, she did not believe in the least in the peace and happiness of Fenella's life. She felt that she was not only unhappy, but frightened. She remembered what Fenella had said about money. 'We've too much . . .' Such an extraordinary thing to say. And the way that she had looked out into the passage, in case she had been overheard . . . In the darkness Caroline found an inexplicable feeling of nervous dread growing in her until she was in such a tense state that she got up and went to the window, trying to calm herself down by watching the black and silver dappling of cloud and moonlight move across the downs.

She had always thought that the trouble with Fenella was that whenever she wanted anything, she wanted it too much, wanted it so that the thought of it filled her whole life for the time being, and nothing else counted at all. So failure, if it came, resulted in unbearable disappointment, while success was almost worse, a dreary, incomprehensible let-down. As she had drifted from job to job and in and out of love-affairs, Caroline had privately believed that a lucky marriage was the only hope for her. And it would need luck, for she was hopelessly without discrimination.

Luck. Caroline remembered how Harry had

harped on the word, but unhappily she found herself doubting that he and Fenella had been good luck for each other.

CHAPTER THREE

In spite of what Caroline felt that night, she became quite sure during the next few days that if Harry was bad luck for Fenella, it was not because he did not love her enough. If she was not happy, and if at times she seemed to be in that odd, scared state that Caroline had noticed on her first afternoon in the guesthouse, it could not be because she was afraid that her husband did not care for her.

If ever Caroline had seen a case of a man in love with his wife, it was Harry Lyddon. Whenever he and Fenella were in a room together, he could hardly make himself look away from her. He feasted his eyes on her, those strange, slightly bulging, brilliantly blue eyes. He seldom went close to her or touched her while anyone else was present, yet it was easy to see that the whole vitality of his small, intensely vigorous body was concentrated upon her. When he impatiently ordered her about, or mocked her, as he often did, it was like a hungry embrace. And whenever he was alone with Caroline, he talked about Fenella, questioned Caroline about her, wanted endlessly to be told what Fenella had been like as a child, as a young girl. Sometimes he even wanted to know what the two of them had been talking about while he was out of the room.

At the same time, Caroline discovered that Fenella had been right when she said that he was kind. It was usually an impulsive kindness, a flash of generosity that perhaps did not cost him much, but still he enjoyed giving pleasure, and his tight little leathery face lit up with charm when he was sure that he had succeeded. He tried hard to find what dishes would tempt Caroline's weak appetite. He brought her books and magazines from Rudbourne. He took her for drives down to the sea and up through the hills and the pretty villages in the neighbourhood. He did his best to amuse her.

This, at times, had a way of being rather maliciously at the expense of other people. However, she decided to do as Fenella had told her and not take too seriously the things that Harry said. He was always ready to put himself out for the people whom he had just been ridiculing. If neither of the other people staying in the guesthouse seemed to want to have much to do with him, it appeared to be because, in their different ways, they were both people who kept themselves to themselves, and not because they felt that he did not do his best for them.

Certainly they both enjoyed his cooking. Mrs. Dewhurst used to sit down at the table with a little sigh of anticipation and ask, 'And what treat have you for us tonight, Mr. Lyddon?'

Food appeared to be one of her only deep interests. She was a widow of about fifty, small and soft and plump, had her hair dyed black, wore a dazzling pink and white makeup and very brightly coloured clothes, and nearly always looked as if she had just got ready to go out to a party. Yet in fact she spent most of her time alone in her room, watching the television set that she had hired in Rudbourne, and hardly ever going out, except for a short walk before lunch to give herself an appetite.

The other guest, Mr. Sherwin, was a slight, middle-aged man with thick spectacles and a dry voice and a rather formal manner, which made him seem older than he probably was. Caroline's first impression of him was of a lean figure darting upstairs to avoid being entrapped in introductions and conversation with the new arrival. But like Mrs. Dewhurst, he was generous to Harry with compliments on his cooking, observing one evening that he was wasted in a guesthouse and that if he had bought a pub instead he could be making a great reputation.

'And what then?' Harry said. He had just served them with *carbonnades flammandes*, which, he informed them, sounded fancy, impressed people, but was cheap.

'Then?' Mr. Sherwin said.

'Then what, when I've got the reputation?'

'Oh. Well, I suppose a bigger and better pub. A name known through the world. Riches.'

'Ah no,' Mrs. Dewhurst said as she eagerly sampled the succulent beef, 'I don't believe Mr. Lyddon's interested in riches. What he loves is this beautiful old house—don't you, Mr. Lyddon? And using his wonderful talents. And the peace and quiet and freedom.'

'Oddly enough, you're quite right,' Harry said. 'And the fact that we can get rid of you all and have it to ourselves as soon as we really want to. That's to say, as soon as my luck turns.'

'But you're so lucky now,' Mrs. Dewhurst said. 'So very lucky, you and your dear wife. You've got almost everything.'

'Except an eager publisher breathing down my neck,' said Harry.

'Ah, you don't know how lucky you are.' She looked from Harry to Fenella with a sentimental smile and her mild grey eyes filled with tears.

They often did this, Caroline had seen, and had learnt, like the others, not to take much notice. But it had helped to give her a certain dread of Mrs. Dewhurst's company. The little widow had quickly taken a liking to her and often came to sit wherever she happened to be, starting a rambling conversation in a soft, flat voice, which always seemed to be leading up to a momentous confidence, but which never got there. Instead she would fall silent and sit staring into space, while the tears welled up. Caroline felt dreadfully sorry for her, and gave what sympathy she could, but found it, day after day, a fearful strain. She was very grateful to Harry when he realised what was happening and came to rescue her.

'I'm sorry about Mrs. Dewhurst,' he said to her one day when he was driving into Rudbourne to the weekly market. 'It's just your bad luck that she's taken such a fancy to you.'

'It isn't that I mind her,' Caroline answered, 'but she's one of the people who drain all the energy out of you.'

Harry nodded. 'Parasitic. Fenella and I had our phase of being very sorry for her, but now I wish to God we weren't stuck with her. But we can't pretend we need her room for somebody else. What do you think of Hugh Sherwin?'

'I've hardly spoken to him,' Caroline said, 'and I think he's spoken even less to me.'

'Oh, come on now. Gossip's life-blood to a writer and as you know, Fenella can't gossip. She doesn't notice other people enough to be able to tell you anything useful about them. So tell me what you really think of Sherwin.'

'Why, are you going to write about him?'

she asked.

'When do I get time to write, feeding your ever-open mouths?'

'But I told you, I don't know him at all. I imagine it would take years and years to get to know him.'

Harry gave a bark of laughter. 'You frighten me with your fearful indiscretion, Caroline. One day you'll make a really dangerous revelation and spend your life regretting it.'

'But I don't even know what he does when he goes into Rudbourne every morning. What does he do there?'

'Do you mean you haven't heard about the bookshop and the fire?'

'No.'

'But I've seen you talking to each other.'

'He doesn't talk much about himself.'

'What does he talk about?'

'Oh, the weather. And once, I think, about old books, but I didn't realise he was in it professionally. Tell me about it.'

'Well, he used to run a second-hand bookshop in Rudbourne and live in a flat over it, but one day last autumn there was a fire and the place was gutted. He was away at the time, at a book sale in London. Has he really never said anything about this?'

'No.'

'It's supposed to have been a fault in the electric wiring that started the fire.'

She turned her head to look at him. 'Why

do you say, "It's *supposed* to have been—" in that tone of voice?'

'Was there something special about my tone of voice? I just meant it's the sort of thing it's apparently very difficult to find out for certain. There's been a detective on the job, asking a lot of questions.'

'If you mean they think he had something to do with it . . .' Caroline considered the idea for a moment, recalling the bookseller's rather pallid face, abrupt voice and stiff, retiring manner, and his one outburst of enthusiasm about old books, which she had found disconcerting but charming. 'No, I'm sure he had nothing to do with it,' she said. 'I like him. I like Mrs. Dewhurst too and I'm awfully sorry for her.'

'Why are you sorry for her?' Harry asked.

'Aren't you?'

'Because she's supposed to be grieving so for the late Mr. Dewhurst?'

'And because she's so lonely that she dresses herself up as she does. She knows she ought to be making a new life for herself, but when it comes to the point, she hasn't the courage to try. It makes her absurd, which is always pathetic when a person's unhappy.'

'So that's how you've got it worked out, is it?'

Caroline knew from his voice that it was not how Harry had worked it out.

'Well,' she said, 'what are your own ideas

35

about her?'

'Oh, I haven't any, I've just a number of questions to ask,' he answered. 'For instance, who and what was Mr. Dewhurst?'

'Hasn't she ever told you?'

'No, and isn't that rather curious? She's lived with us for six months and never told us anything about him. She's never told us what he did for a living. She's never told us how he died.'

'Perhaps he isn't dead. Perhaps they just separated.'

'That's a thought. And she's waiting all dolled up for the day he comes back to her. But why shouldn't she go out a little in the meantime? As I said, Fenella and I used to feel sorry for her and used to try to take her out for an occasional drink or cinema. D'you think she'd come? Never. When I suggested it, she looked as frightened as if she thought I was going to assault her.'

The car had reached the chalk cutting. Ahead the road wound down into the village. Each day the valley grew a little greener, and more white blossom appeared on the blackthorns that crouched in twisted shapes on the smooth hillsides. The roofs of Rudbourne showed in the hazy distance. The sky was clear and there was sunshine everywhere.

'So I ask myself,' Harry went on, 'is she frightened, perhaps—I mean, frightened of something real, like being recognised?'

Caroline began to laugh. 'Oh, Harry, I believe you're trying to tell me you think she murdered poor Mr. Dewhurst!'

Harry gave a swift grin that tightened the deep lines in his brown, leathery cheeks.

'Sure I'm not serious, Caroline?'

'About as serious as you were when you suggested Mr. Sherwin burnt his shop down to collect the insurance.'

'Why do you think I wasn't serious about that?'

'Look,' she said, 'it's a lovely morning. Why spoil it?'

Harry shook his head. 'If you'd been a crime reporter for a dozen years, as I was, you'd be saying to yourself that far stranger things happen than arson committed by a respectable bookseller. Arson's an awfully common crime, and Sherwin got a tidy sum, you know, for a lot of books he might never have been able to sell. That story about the defective wiring too— mightn't it be just a tiny bit thin and worth looking into? And husbands have died from the arsenic in the cocoa given to them by their loving wives.'

'I've an idea,' Caroline said thoughtfully, 'that the trouble with you is that really you're hankering to go back to that job of crime reporting.'

'You're still sure I'm not serious, aren't you?' He gave her one of his hard, brilliant glances. 'What about the detective then? I'm not making him up. He came round last week, asking a lot of questions. At least, a man came and asked a lot of questions.'

'About Mr. Sherwin?'

'Actually about everyone in the place.'

'What sort of questions?'

'How long we'd known them, what we thought about them and so on.'

'Did he ask about Mrs. Dewhurst?'

'Oh yes, and about the daily help from the village and about Jan Pullen.'

'Who's he?'

'He runs the garage at the corner. Which reminds me, I want to stop in for some petrol.'

'And what's his line in crime?'

Harry laughed. 'All right, I know you don't believe a word I'm saying. Honestly, however, I wouldn't mind knowing what Jan's doing in a garage like that, hammering away half the night. Haven't you heard him? The sound carries because of some queer echo from the hills. You can get much nearer to the place and not hear anything.'

Caroline nodded, remembering the distant metallic hammering that had helped to keep her awake when she first came to the guesthouse. She had heard the noise once or twice since then, but like the other disconnected sounds of night-time in the country, it no longer disturbed her.

'And what's a man like Jan doing,' Harry went on, slowing down as they came in sight of the little garage at the fork in the road, 'running this sort of place at all?'

'What's wrong with him?' she asked.

'You'll see, I shan't have to tell you.' He turned the car in at the garage, pulling up behind a van that was at the petrol pumps ahead of them.

While they waited there, Caroline inquired, 'What was the man like who asked the questions, Harry? And what did you tell him?'

'I don't know what he was like, I didn't see him,' he said. 'Fenella saw him. And what she told him . . .' He shrugged his shoulders. 'Perhaps all the secrets of her heart. Or nothing. She says she told him nothing. But that was the day she decided she had to go to London to see you. Suddenly, you know, after two years. Do you still think I'm joking, Caroline?'

If he was, Caroline was beginning not to like the joke.

'She didn't mention the man to me,' she said.

'Perhaps because of finding you ill. Or perhaps because there wasn't any man after all. I told you I hadn't invented him, but it's possible Fenella . . .'

He stopped. The van ahead was moving on and the young man who had been attending to it came towards the car, saying, 'Hello, Harry.'

Even those two words told Caroline what Harry thought was wrong with him. His accent was wrong. His manner was wrong. The parents who had paid, probably expensively, for his education, could never have dreamt that it would lead him merely to running a small country garage.

Apart from that, however, there were no obvious reasons to find fault with him. He was tall and well made. He had a dark, lively face and thick dark hair. His rolled-up sleeves showed muscular forearms.

'Four of the usual?' he asked.

'Yes, please, Jan.' Getting out of the car, Harry introduced him to Caroline, telling him that she was Fenella's sister.

The young man looked at her gravely for a moment, said good-afternoon, then turned away to the pumps. It left her puzzling why she should feel that she had met that steady, thoughtful look before. There had been something in it that seemed extraordinarily familiar. Yet if she had ever met him before, she thought, she would have remembered him. Or had she reached an age when one good-looking young man was beginning to look very much like another?

Whatever the explanation, when he looked at her again a minute or two later, the sense of familiarity had gone.

'Reminds me, I've been wanting to see you, Harry,' he said, as he put the money that Harry had given him into a pocket of his overalls. 'There was a man around here a few

40

days ago, asking questions about you. Pointless questions, they seemed to me, but I thought perhaps you ought to know.'

'Questions about *me*?'

Harry had just got back into the car. Caroline saw his small, powerful hands tense on the wheel.

Jan Pullen nodded. 'Yes, and about Fenella and Mrs. Dewhurst and Mr. Sherwin.'

Harry gave a quick glance at Caroline, then looked back at Jan Pullen.

'What sort of questions? What sort of man?'

'A tough type. About forty. Paunchy, but plenty of muscle. Slightly bald. Curious eyes, not on the same level. Wore a dark business suit, but didn't look as if he were used to wearing it. National Health false teeth. Hands like hams, with the little finger of his left hand bent, as if he'd broken it sometime.'

'How very observant you are, Mr. Pullen,' Caroline remarked, wondering if, in the penetrating, assessing glance that he had given her when they met, he had taken in as many details of her appearance.

'By God, he is!' Harry's face had turned dark red. For no reason that Caroline could understand, there was hatred in his voice. And it was hatred of Jan Pullen, that was what was puzzling about it, not of the man who had been asking questions. 'What did he ask you, Jan? Is your memory any good about that?'

'Probably not,' Pullen answered. 'He

rambled a good deal. Wanted to know how long you and Fenella had been here and what you'd done before. Said he was thinking of taking a holiday here. That didn't strike me as likely. I didn't think he was a type that'd care for a holiday in Dexter Abbas.'

'And what did you tell him about us all?' Harry asked.

'I said it was a fine day.'

'In answer to everything he asked you?'

'There are all sorts of ways of saying it's a fine day, Harry. I used them all.'

'I'll bet!' Harry muttered and abruptly sent the car shooting forward.

For the next few minutes he drove wildly. He drove too fast, cut corners and scowled at the road ahead as if it were a malevolent creature that he was flattening out of existence. When Caroline spoke to him he did not answer. He was concentrating completely on his mysterious fury. She doubted if he had even heard her.

But presently he had to slow down because he had caught up with the van that had been at the garage before them. It took up so much of the narrow road that for the moment there was no hope of passing it.

Cursing the delay, though in itself it was quite unimportant, he said, 'Well, what did you make of that, Caroline?'

'Oh, he's unusual,' she answered. 'But is there anything more unusual about him than about a crime reporter who does the cooking at a guesthouse?'

Harry gave her a sardonic glance. 'You know that isn't what I was asking. I want to know, what did you make of his story? What did you make of the tough type with the hands like hams and the broken little finger? A nice touch, that.'

'I'm sorry, Harry, I don't understand,' she said. 'You seemed to think perhaps Fenella invented the man. Now you know she didn't. Why should that make you so angry with Jan Pullen?'

The driver of the van was signalling for them to pass. Harry speeded up for a moment, decided not to risk it and dropped behind again.

'Because of that damned little finger!' he exclaimed. 'Because of the paunch and the hands like hams. Shall I tell you what Fenella said he was like? She said he was small and nervous-looking, with a pale, foxy face.'

'Then there must have been two men.'

Harry gave a snort of derision.

'Well, why not?' she asked. 'Detectives often hunt in couples, don't they?'

'Detectives!'

'Isn't that what they are? You said—'

'God knows what they are!' he snarled through his teeth. 'But I'll find out. They needn't think I won't.'

The van driver had slowed down to give

them a chance to pass and was signalling again with growing impatience. The road ahead was clear. Harry accelerated.

What happened next remained a terrifying confusion in Caroline's mind. Afterwards she could remember the high, smooth side of the van swaying towards them. She remembered the face of the driver. His lips were drawn back and his jaw was working, but she could not hear what he was shouting. She could hear nothing but the high scream of skidding tyres. Somehow she never felt the shock of the collision itself. It was blotted out of her memory as completely as if it had never occurred. Yet she remembered the feeling of the car moving sideways, and then, with an unearthly sort of slow-motion, beginning to turn over.

CHAPTER FOUR

It was Harry who saved them. Before the van slammed into them, he put the car into a sideways skid, which lessened the force of the blow and meant that they only went sliding into the ditch, where thick bushes made a springy cushion under the car as it toppled. If he had been slower, if he had tried to keep the car on the road a moment longer, they would have been hurled straight at the thick trunk of a tree and almost certainly been crushed to death.

That, at least, was how a police sergeant, almost awestruck with admiration for Harry's presence of mind, later explained it to Caroline.

At the time it simply seemed to her that a miracle had happened. There had been a moment when her world had fallen apart in crazy fragments, and the face of death, uncommonly like that of the van-driver who had vanished, had stared wildly at her out of the whirling chaos. Then she was somehow merely lying in an extremely uncomfortable position, with a feeling of numbness making her stupid and helpless, while Harry, loquacious with shock but still keeping his head, was trying to haul her clear of the wrecked car, and telling her over and over again how lucky she was, how damned lucky.

The person who was out of luck, he went on, panting and straining, was the murdering drunk in the van, because Harry was going to get him. If it was the last thing he ever did, Harry was going to get him. And after that the man would never drive again. And there were a lot of other things the man would never do again. More and more such things occurred to Harry as Caroline emerged from the car and the two of them rather suddenly sat down on the grass by the roadside, where Mr. Sherwin, driving back from Rudbourne, presently found them.

As he stopped his car and jumped out, Harry lurched on to his feet. By that time his concern for Caroline had been wholly replaced by his concern to trace the van, to start, while his blood was hot, his dire revenge on the driver.

'A van did it—a green van,' he cried. 'Have you seen it?'

'One thing at a time.' The bookseller's voice was as crisp and precise as ever. 'Are you hurt, Miss Dyer?'

Harry answered for her, 'She's nearly dead. So am I. But my car's quite dead. Dead and done for—my new car! I've only had it a month. God, when I get my hands on him . . .! You must have passed him, Sherwin. A green van, swaying about the road, driven by a drunk.'

Mr. Sherwin stooped over Caroline. 'Can you move?' he asked. 'Can you get as far as my car?'

'I don't think I'm actually hurt at all,' she said, 'except in my feelings.'

'That's good,' he said briskly. 'Then the sooner we get you home the better. Let me help.'

He held out his hands to her. She grasped them and stood up.

At once darkness closed in on her. For an instant almost everything was blotted out. Only the spectacled face, close to hers, remained positively there, did not fade. It was a face that she had hardly noticed before, but for that moment in which it became the only link that she had with consciousness, seemed to possess an almost godlike strength. Then the faintness passed. She walked to the car. She was only a little unsteady.

Following her, Harry said, 'I know what we'll do, we'll stop and ask Pullen if he knows him.'

'Now, do you mean?' Mr. Sherwin asked.

'Yes,' Harry said. 'The man was buying petrol just ahead of us. He may be a regular customer.'

'I don't think we'd better stop, all the same,' Mr. Sherwin said. 'I think the first thing to do is to get Miss Dyer home—then get a doctor and the police, in that order.'

'We can stop just for a moment,' Harry said. 'Even if Jan doesn't know the man, he may have noticed the number on the van.'

'Home first,' Mr. Sherwin said stubbornly.

If there was nothing about him now which Caroline, feeling more herself again, any longer found godlike, she felt immensely grateful for the fact that he had sufficient strength of will to cope with Harry.

But Harry was never much inclined to give in to others. When they reached the garage he exclaimed, 'Damn it, it'll only take a minute!'

Mr. Sherwin drove straight on.

'You can telephone from the house,' he

said.

'But Caroline won't mind stopping—will you, Caroline?' Harry pleaded.

'The telephone will do just as well,' Mr. Sherwin answered in his level voice.

However, as soon as they reached the house, it was he, getting out of the car and darting indoors far faster than Harry was expecting, who took possession of the telephone, and while Harry fumed at his elbow, rang up a doctor and the police. Harry did not actually snatch the instrument away from him, but all the time that Mr. Sherwin was talking, he kept talking too, taking no notice of Fenella, who had come running into the room and was begging to be told what had happened.

'If you think it over,' Harry said feverishly, 'Jan must have seen the man was drunk. Drunk and dangerous. He'd no damned right to give him petrol. It was a crime. He'd no damned right to take his money. It was a crime almost as bad as the other man's. Worse, because he knew what he was doing. Just wait till I tell him what I think of him!'

In a voice that became quieter the more excited Harry's became, Mr. Sherwin finished talking on the telephone, told Harry to calm down and let the police handle things in their own way, directed Fenella to make Caroline go to bed, and said that he himself was returning to the scene of the accident to keep watch over the car until the police arrived there.

Harry showed no sign of trying to calm down. Before Mr. Sherwin was out of the room, he was shouting excitedly into the telephone.

Fenella turned to Caroline. There were tears of fright in her voice.

'But what *did* happen? What's Jan *done*?'

'Let's go upstairs,' Caroline suggested.

'Oh yes, of course.' Fenella put an arm round her. 'But I can't understand—why is Harry so angry with Jan?'

'I think it's just shock,' Caroline said. 'He was wonderful when the accident happened.'

'But what had Jan to do with it? Was it something he did to the car? It can't be. It's brand new, he hasn't had a chance to do anything at all to it.'

Caroline was confusedly remembering that Harry had been angry with Jan Pullen before the accident. She couldn't at the moment remember just why. Whatever it had been, it seemed too complicated to say anything about it now. Besides, Harry had been angry with Fenella too, which it would be a silly thing to mention.

'It's reaction, he's just blowing off steam,' she said. 'At the time he was so calm. He kept his head perfectly.'

'He's always wonderful in a crisis,' Fenella said. 'He can think so fast. He's awfully brave too. I once saw him dive straight off a bridge

49

into a river in all his clothes . . . Oh, I told you about that, didn't I?' She opened the door of Caroline's bedroom. 'Now do please try to tell me what happened. I've simply got to know.'

Caroline was beginning to feel her bruises and her head was swimming again. She kicked off her shoes and lay down on the bed.

'I can't tell you much,' she said, 'except that we were behind a van and the driver signalled us to pass, and when we did, the van swung out and hit us. I think the driver was drunk, as Harry says.'

'Did you see the man?'

'I seem to remember his face at the window. He was making awful faces at us. I think he was as terrified as we were.'

'Did you see whose van it was? Was there a name on it?'

'There may have been. I don't remember.'

'But where does Jan come in?'

'Harry wanted to know if he knew the man. We saw the van first at his garage.'

'Then Jan had nothing at all to do with it.'

'Nothing, except that he gave the man petrol. Harry seems to think he'd no right to do that.'

'Because the man was drunk?'

'Yes.'

'But he may not even have realised it. If his mind was on something else . . .' Fenella smiled. Most of the worry had faded from her long, pale face. 'Harry'll calm down soon. Now

50

I'm sure you ought to get into bed properly, not just lie there.'

Caroline gave a groan. She had a horror of having to go back to bed at this stage in her general recovery. She had been getting on so well. It was a matter of pride not to collapse again.

When she did not stir, Fenella flapped her long, helpless-looking hands at her.

'At least get those clothes off,' she said. 'They're a mess. Come on, I'll help you.'

'It's all right, I can manage,' Caroline said. It had just dawned on her that nearly all Fenella's anxiety, the tears in her voice and her pallor, had been for Jan. With it allayed, she had time to concern herself with her sister's condition.

'Oh, come on now.'

Fenella slid an arm under her and pulled her up. Her hands were much stronger, much firmer than they looked. Like her will, Caroline thought, as she allowed her clothes to be pulled off. When Fenella wanted something, she went after it. Nothing would ever stop her. Nothing ever had, that Caroline could remember. She had a complete indifference to consequences, probably could not even imagine them.

'There, that's better,' Fenella said, wrapping Caroline in her dressing-gown and covering her with the eiderdown. 'But isn't it terrible, you come here to get well and we do this to you . . . ?' She turned her head away, listening. 'There's a car. I expect it's the doctor.'

She went out quickly.

Shutting her eyes, Caroline went on thinking about Fenella, about Jan Pullen, who was so big, so good-looking, who, if he had come to meet the train at Rudbourne, she would have picked out instantly as Fenella's husband. Well, if Fenella had fallen in love with him, if she wanted him, she would have him. Harry would just have to put up with it.

Only it was difficult to imagine Harry putting up with anything that he did not like. Caroline wondered what Fenella thought about that.

The door opened quietly. Thinking that the doctor had been astonishingly quick at getting up the stairs, Caroline opened her eyes again and saw, not the doctor, but Mrs. Dewhurst tiptoeing across the room towards her.

'I don't want to disturb you, dear,' she said in a low voice, 'but I had to find out how you were. I heard them talking about an accident, the doctor, the police. Then I saw Mrs. Lyddon helping you upstairs. Are you much hurt, dear? Tell me what happened.'

Caroline felt an enormous weariness descend on her. She thought of having to tell the doctor what had happened, then the police, then, for all she knew, a reporter from the local paper, then perhaps more reporters, more and more . . .

52

The room was spinning. It spun round Mrs. Dewhurst, whose bright red dress began to balloon into a blood-coloured cloud.

'I'm quite all right, thank you, Mrs. Dewhurst,' Caroline said, hoping that this would make the cloud go away. 'Nothing happened.'

Mrs. Dewhurst came closer.

'Call me Emma,' she said. 'I wish you would.'

'Emma. Nothing happened. Just a little accident. Nothing at all.'

Caroline could hear Mrs. Dewhurst's heavy breathing near her face. Why, she thought in surprise, she's really worried about me, she's really upset.

'Please, dear,' Mrs. Dewhurst whispered, 'try to tell me, what was he like, the driver of the other car?'

Her soft, round face was so near to Caroline that she could smell the cream and powder on it. No part of it moved when Mrs. Dewhurst spoke, except for her brilliant lips, which writhed together like two little red worms.

'Did you see him?' she breathed into Caroline's ear.

'I'd only a glimpse of him,' Caroline said.

'Would you know him again?'

'I don't know.'

'And what were you wearing?'

The question was so unexpected that Caroline thought that she could not have heard it correctly. 'What was I . . . ?'

'Yes,' Mrs. Dewhurst whispered eagerly. 'Was it your coat, your blue coat?'

'Yes, as a matter of fact, it was,' Caroline said. 'Why? What difference does it make?'

'Oh, none, dear. I just wondered. It's such a pretty coat, I hope it wasn't spoilt.'

There were voices in the corridor.

'Now here's the doctor,' Mrs. Dewhurst said. 'I must go. I do hope I haven't tired you. I was just so worried about you.'

'Thank you, Mrs. Dewhurst, it's very kind of you.'

'Emma, please.'

'Emma.'

She patted Caroline's shoulder with a plump little hand and as Fenella and the doctor came into the room, murmured apologies for being in the way and sidled hurriedly out.

The doctor examined Caroline's bruises, dressed a cut on her forehead that she did not know she had, told her that she was lucky and that she should stay in bed and that he would look in at her again next day. Soon after he had gone a police sergeant came and also told her that she was lucky. With Harry, she thought, that made three of them.

'Lucky, lucky me,' she murmured.

'I beg your pardon,' the sergeant said. He was a lean, scrubbed-looking man with a soft voice and an air of generally apologising for his presence.

'It's just that at the moment I find it awfully hard to believe in my luck,' she said.

'That's natural enough,' he said. 'All the same, if Mr. Lyddon hadn't thought so quick . . .'

He went on to tell her about the tree by the roadside, making her realise that she owed her life to Harry's quickness of reaction.

After that he asked her all the questions that she had been expecting. Had she seen the driver of the van? Could she describe him? Had she noticed any name on the van? Had she noticed the number?

She told him what she had told Fenella, while the sergeant made careful notes.

'I reckon we'll pick him up without much trouble,' he said when he put his notebook away. 'I'm not sure but I could put a name to him now.'

'Then he's a local man, is he?' she asked. 'Someone who's done it before?'

'Well, I'll know more when I've talked to Mr. Pullen,' he answered noncommittally. 'But you can be sure we'll find him.'

He wished her a quick recovery and left.

For some time after that Caroline rested, because it was what everybody seemed to think that she ought to do. But she made up her mind, in spite of what the doctor had said, that she was not going to have dinner in her room. Until that day she had not really realised how

55

tired she was of trays, of staying in bed, of being ill. And lying there by herself now was not at all soothing, but had a curiously upsetting effect on her. She kept re-living the moment before the accident, kept seeing the driver's grimacing face, while all the questions that she had been asked kept pounding on her ear-drums. Did you see him, would you recognise him, why is Harry so angry with Jan, with handsome, beloved Jan, were you wearing your blue coat . . . ?

About seven o'clock she got up, dressed and went downstairs.

Harry heard her on the stairs and came darting out of the sitting-room to meet her.

'Tough, huh?' he said, grinning up at her happily. So far as she could see, all his earlier anger had disappeared. 'That's fine. Thank God I didn't kill you.'

'Kill me? If you hadn't been so quick, Harry—' She tried to start the little speech that she had prepared in which she intended to thank him for kindly saving her life.

His laughter stopped it. Putting an arm round her, he kissed her warmly.

'Come in and join us,' he said. 'We're celebrating. We're drinking to the next of our nine lives—of which, speaking for myself, there can't be so very many left.'

He drew her into the sitting-room.

CHAPTER FIVE

The room was long and narrow. It had once been two rooms, the partition between them having been removed to make one large enough for the visitors who came in the summer. This made the small group who were there now, gathered round the fireplace at the far end of the room, look rather as if they had chosen to sit at the end of a passage. The lamps left unlit near the door and all the unused arm-chairs and coffee tables, helped to give the room the appearance of having been stretched out of shape. But at least at the far end it had an atmosphere of warmth and cheerfulness.

Fenella was sitting on one side of the fire, Emma Dewhurst on the other. Hugh Sherwin was standing at a table, refilling their glasses. Drinks with their boarders before dinner was not a normal ritual of the Lyddons. If they wanted drinks themselves, they generally had them in the kitchen, while Harry was putting the last touches to the meal. But tonight, he repeated, as he led Caroline to the fire, they were celebrating.

'Anyway, I'm celebrating and Caroline's celebrating, whatever the rest of you are doing.' His voice was gay and excited as he picked up his glass. 'Here's to long life and confusion to our enemies.'

'Which is a curious phrase, when you come to think of it, isn't it?' Mr. Sherwin said. 'I'm inclined to think a confused enemy might be a particularly dangerous one. Irrational and unpredictable. I think I'll drink to his clearer thinking.'

'Have it your own way, so long as you don't pretend you haven't any enemies.' Harry drew a chair up to the fire for Caroline, then went to sit beside Fenella. 'What a state to be in— thinking, I mean, that you ought to say that. An enemy gives some point to existence. When you don't know why else you're alive, at least you know it's your job to defeat him.'

Mrs. Dewhurst gave a shocked little cough. She looked as if she were about to speak, then took a nervous sip from her glass instead. She drank in the same way as she spoke, with almost no motion in her face, no sign of swallowing, but only a cautious, nibbling motion of her red lips.

Fenella murmured, 'Oh, Harry, you haven't any enemies.'

She had leant her cheek on her hand and was gazing into the fire. Her thick fair hair hung forward, almost hiding her face.

Harry laughed. 'I've dozens, darling. Well, half a dozen. Or one or two or three.'

'You only imagine them,' she said.

He moved closer to her. He did not touch her, but with his sheer concentration upon her he might have been holding her tight.

'Then why d'you think we're here?' he asked.

'Here?' she said uncertainly. 'Tonight, you mean?'

'No, in Dexter Abbas, in this house. Why d'you think I gave up my job, if it wasn't that things were getting too hot for me?'

'Oh, Harry . . .' she said with a little shake of her head.

'No, I mean it.' His voice was solemn, but there was still a spark of laughter in his eyes. 'A crime reporter, if he knows his job, finds out far too many things for his own good. Things the police never hear about. Things that never get into his paper. So a time comes when, if he's wise, he lets the news go round that he's getting out. He sees to it that certain people hear he's lost all interest in their activities. That's supposing he's happily married and finds life worth living.'

'You know you gave up your job because you wanted to do some serious writing,' Fenella said.

'My God, whatever else it is, when I get around to it,' Harry said, 'I hope it won't be serious.'

'Well, you know what I mean,' she said.

Mr. Sherwin said, 'I shouldn't try arguing with your husband tonight, Mrs. Lyddon. You can allow him to be a bit fey for once. He's earned it.'

'Fey!' Harry cried. 'You're calling me fey? Do you know the real meaning of that word?'

'Why?' Mr. Sherwin asked. 'Is there something wrong with it?'

'It means acting unnaturally, as if doomed to calamity or death.'

The eyes behind the bookseller's thick spectacles widened slightly. 'I'm very sorry, Lyddon, I'd no such thought in my mind. I was thinking rather of a state of—well, euphoria, resulting naturally from having escaped death.'

Caroline's head was throbbing uncomfortably. She wondered why she had had the silly idea of coming downstairs, but since she was here, she felt that she ought to say something, not sit quite silent, like a ghost at the feast.

'Do tell us some more about those enemies of yours, Harry,' she said. 'They sound fascinating.'

Mrs. Dewhurst choked over a sip of sherry.

'Oh, please don't—it isn't funny!' she gasped. 'It's a terrible thing to have an enemy.'

But as if he had taken Caroline's request as a challenge to convince them all that he really had enemies, had lots of them, went daily in fear of his life, Harry sprang to his feet with his small, leathery face suddenly drawn and angry. It was an amazingly realistic performance, Caroline thought hazily. The anger looked just like real anger.

'I'm not joking, I'm serious, dead serious,'

he cried. 'Don't you understand, I know too much about too many people? Dangerous people! And after what happened today, I know that somebody wants me out of the way.'

Mr. Sherwin glanced quickly at Caroline, then looked soberly down at the glass in his hand.

'Who would that be, I wonder,' he said.

'If I knew, do you think I'd have walked into that trap today?' Harry demanded furiously. 'And with Caroline in the car! Would I ever have given them a chance to pull a crude trick like that?'

'I understood from Sergeant Rutter that the van-driver was probably one of our local drunks,' Mr. Sherwin said. 'Troublesome but not sinister.'

'He wasn't drunk,' Harry said more quietly, but very positively. 'He knew just what he was doing. He signalled us to pass, then smashed into us. Ask Caroline. Ask Jan Pullen, if you don't believe us.'

Fenella lifted her head. 'What did Jan tell you, Harry?'

'That he was sure the man wasn't drunk when he was at the garage.'

'He could have been mistaken,' Fenella said.

'Yes, but he also said he'd never seen the man before. And not only to me. He said the same to Rutter.' Harry tilted himself back on his heels, staring up at the low ceiling. 'I wasn't really suspicious till I heard that,' he said.

'I don't suppose Pullen knows all the drunks in the neighbourhood,' Mr. Sherwin said.

'He wasn't drunk,' Harry repeated. 'And Jan knew him. And I'm not sure that isn't the most interesting part of the whole affair, the fact that Jan obviously knows him quite well.'

'I don't understand,' Fenella said apprehensively. 'How can you tell that Jan knows him?'

'I've listened to a lot of statements, made by a lot of people,' Harry said. 'One gets a habit of spotting a lie.'

Hugh Sherwin was frowning, as if he had lost his liking for the conversation.

'You didn't say any of this to the police when they were here, did you?' he said.

'Can you imagine what Rutter would have made of it? No,' Harry said, 'let him go on looking for the drunk in the plain van. I've taken other steps to protect myself, as it happens. I took them long ago. I put everything dangerous I know about anybody on to paper. It's all written down. So if anything happens to me, there it is.'

'Where?' Fenella asked.

At the same moment Mrs. Dewhurst got unsteadily to her feet. Her face was working unnaturally. She looked near tears.

'I'm sorry, I don't like this,' she said. 'It upsets me. I can't go on listening. You're a very foolish young man, Mr. Lyddon. Very foolish.'

Knocking over her glass as she went, sending it rolling across the hearthrug, she went hurrying away between the empty chairs and the little coffee tables towards the distant door.

Mr. Sherwin caught up with her before she reached it, took her by the arm and drew her round.

'Come, you know Lyddon too well to take him seriously,' he said. 'Make allowances for the accident. He's still excited, but he'll calm down presently.'

He looked back at Harry as he said it. Harry met the look, shrugged his shoulders and grinned.

'Sorry, Mrs. Dewhurst, of course I was only fooling,' he said. 'Joke over. It was a poor joke. I haven't an enemy in the world.'

He dropped back on to the sofa beside Fenella.

She jerked away from him. It was only the smallest of movements. Harry gave no sign that he had seen it. Caroline saw it only out of the corner of her eye while she was watching Mr. Sherwin and Mrs. Dewhurst return to their chairs, but it made her turn her head to look at Fenella.

She was looking straight at Caroline, looking at her with staring, imploring eyes. There were agony and terror on her long, lovely horse-face.

'Help me,' her look said. 'For God's sake, help me. You've known me all my life, you're the only one who can help. It's why I went to London to fetch you.'

Then she looked down into the fire again and her fair hair swung forward across her cheek.

Caroline felt her heart start pounding, as if Fenella's fear had been poured straight into her own veins. Yet she had no understanding at all of where the fear came from. Was it fear of Harry, or fear for Harry, or really nothing to do with Harry? While Harry had been talking about his mysterious enemies and claiming that the accident in the afternoon had been an attempt on his life, Fenella had looked merely exasperated, merely mildly desperate. Yet now, when he had promised to stop his nonsense, she looked as if her whole world had just crashed about her in ruins.

But there was nothing that Caroline could do for her just then, for a few minutes later Harry swept them all in to dinner, and for the next half hour there was nothing for it but to act as if she had noticed nothing. It was an uneasy time. Harry's high spirit had abruptly run out. He sat at the end of the table, looking shrunken and exhausted and withdrawn into himself. Mrs. Dewhurst was at her most silent and vacant-faced. Mr. Sherwin made one or two attempts to cheer Harry up, as if to make amends for having spoilt his mood, but was far less successful than he had been in quelling him.

Thinking of the ease with which he had done that, Caroline found herself beginning to wonder a good deal what other powers might be kept in reserve by the stooping, quiet man. If he could be so formidable when he chose, what else did he conceal behind his thick spectacles and precise manner? What was he like when he forgot to keep people at a distance? Or did he never lose his formality and, for instance, call them by their Christian names? She wondered what sort of people his friends were, if he had any, or if he was a true solitary, with no interest in life but the old books that had been burnt.

For that evening, at least, he seemed to have had enough of involving himself in other people's affairs, for as soon as the meal was over he darted upstairs to his room.

Caroline decided to copy him and, catching Fenella's eye, said deliberately that she was too tired to stay downstairs any longer and was going up to bed. As she expected, Fenella said immediately that she would bring her coffee up to her.

When she appeared with it, ten minutes later, Caroline was walking restlessly about her bedroom, smoking a cigarette, a thing that she did only rarely, but which, just then, helped her to feel that she could cope with Fenella, could listen with patience and control her own nerves.

When Fenella saw her, she said in surprise, 'Not in bed yet?'

Caroline had decided not to waste subtlety on her.

'Well now, you'd better tell me everything, hadn't you?' she said. 'I can't be much use to you till I know what it's all about.'

Fenella shut the door behind her, put the coffee down on a table, sat down on the nearest chair and began to cry.

Caroline prowled about the room, taking sharp puffs at her cigarette. She was not in the least startled by Fenella's tears. This scene was one that they had enacted quite often in the past and Caroline knew more or less how it would go. The general lines of it were always the same, even if the details varied. Fenella had to give way to her tears and Caroline had to wait while they poured, or Fenella would never be able to talk about what was troubling her. For as long as she tried to control herself, she would stay evasive and inarticulate and might go away with her burden as mysteriously oppressive as ever.

But this time she started fighting her tears almost at once.

'I mustn't do this,' she muttered. 'I don't want them to see I've been crying. That's the worst of having people here all the time. They always see everything.'

Mopping her eyes, she got up and went to

the dressing-table, peering at herself in the mirror, then dabbing some of Caroline's powder on to her face.

She went on, 'I've been waiting and hoping you'd start talking, Caroline, but you seemed to have made up your mind not to say anything.'

'You've been waiting for *me* . . .?' Caroline said. 'What on earth have you been expecting?'

'That you'd tell me what you thought about him.'

'About Harry?'

'Yes, of course.'

'But why? It's what *you* think of him that counts, isn't it?'

Fenella gave a sigh. 'Of course, you aren't married,' she observed. 'Perhaps you don't realise . . . What I mean is, he's such a mixture, Caroline.'

'Yes, married or not, it's quite easy to see that. Well?'

'And he isn't at all the sort of man I used to fall in love with. I've never felt I knew where I was with him, and I don't suppose I ever shall. But he swept me off my feet somehow. He's so much more—well, more alive than most people.'

'Yes, I can see all that. But I don't understand what's gone wrong? What's Harry done?'

'I don't know exactly, that's just it.'

'Do you mean he hasn't done anything, and you're the one . . .?' Caroline paused. She realised that she did not want to seem to have been watching, to have noticed too much. She would not, she resolved, mention the name of Jan Pullen.

'No, it isn't me,' Fenella said. She went back to the chair, dropped into it wearily and stared into the middle-distance. 'It's Harry, but I'm not sure that it's exactly his *fault*. It's just the queer way he looks at things, his whole attitude to everything and everybody. Look at the things he says about other people. He seems to think everyone's hiding something awful.'

'Oh, that. That's just his rather odd sort of humour, isn't it?'

'Do you think so?'

'Don't you?'

'Oh, he always turns it into a joke if you argue with him,' Fenella said. 'And that's just when I feel most sure he means every word of it.'

'Ah,' Caroline said, beginning to understand a little, 'as he did tonight?'

'Yes, it was when he started laughing it off that I began to think he really believes he's got enemies who want to kill him.'

'And are you more afraid that he has, or that he hasn't?'

'I don't think he's mad, if that's what you mean.'

'Well, that's something.'

Yet Fenella had spoken with a casualness which had sent an unpleasant chill through Caroline. It seemed that there was nothing unfamiliar, nothing shocking to Fenella in the suggestion that her husband might be mad.

'But I don't think he ever completely trusts anybody,' she went on. 'Even people he likes. And that isn't normal exactly, is it?'

'I suppose not,' said Caroline.

'And it's got me into such a muddle, I don't know whom I trust and whom I don't. And that isn't like me, is it? You've always said I accept people at their face-value far too easily.'

'Oh dear, the things I seem to have said . . .'

'But it's quite true, I do. So now, when I find I've stopped trusting him . . .' Fenella picked up a fold of her skirt between finger and thumb and began to pinch and wrestle with it.

Caroline said, 'If you're afraid he's anything but madly in love with you, you can stop worrying about that this minute.'

Fenella frowned as if the interruption had been quite meaningless.

'You see, sometimes I get the feeling there must be a real reason for the things he says,' she went on, 'but then I start wondering about him. About his past and where he's picked up the sort of things he knows.'

'I should have thought twelve years of reporting explains that,' Caroline said.

She saw Fenella had not even heard her.

'A thing happened last week, Caroline—it's really why I went to London to see you,' she said. 'A man came here, asking questions about him. He pretended to be asking about a lot of other people too, but I'm sure it was Harry he really wanted to know about. I told Harry about him and he just laughed in that excited sort of way he has. So then I got scared and decided I'd got to talk to somebody and I thought of you. But I found you were ill, so it didn't seem right to bother you with it. Then I thought the best thing would be for you to come here and meet Harry and be able to make up your mind about him for yourself.'

'And today he goes and saves my life.' Caroline went to Fenella's side and laid a hand on her hair for a moment. 'I don't think I'm going to find it very easy to be objective about him, Fenella.'

Fenella looked up at her and smiled fleetingly. 'I know. That's what he's like. Quick and fearless. And I love him for it, even if I don't sound as if I do. I really do, Caroline. But he's ruthless too. He says one has to be. He says if you don't trample on other people, they'll trample on you. He's sure of it. And then there's the money problem . . .' She frowned down at her writhing fingers.

'What do you mean?' Caroline asked. 'Haven't things worked out here as you hoped? You told me when I came that you'd plenty of money.'

'Yes, yes, yes!' Fenella cried desperately. 'We have, we've too much money, that's the trouble!'

CHAPTER SIX

Caroline met her sister's eyes with bewilderment. She felt right out of her depth. Sitting down on the edge of her bed, she said, 'I honestly don't understand how that's possible.'

'Oh, I don't mean we've *too much*—no, of course not. But where's it coming from?' Fenella gave an uneasy glance at the closed door then lowered her voice. 'I know how much we're making out of the guesthouse. I keep the accounts, and even if I get them in rather a mess sometimes, I always know more or less how they ought to come out. And I know how much we've got in the bank. We've a joint account, so I can keep an eye on it, and if anything, we always have a little less than I expect, not more—you know how that happens.'

'I do indeed,' said Caroline.

'Well, the guesthouse is doing all right. That's to say, we did very well in the summer and I managed to put some money aside. But through the winter, as I told you, I don't

71

believe it pays us to keep open. At most, we just cover expenses. Yet Harry always has some money. Not an awful lot, but more than makes sense.'

'Haven't you asked him about it?'

'Yes, of course, and he just says casually he's sold an article to some paper.'

'Perhaps that's it, then.'

'But when he has—when he really has, I mean, a letter comes with a cheque in it, and then I see the money in our account. Besides, he hasn't done any writing for a long time. None. We came here, he gave up his job and we started all this, just to give him a chance to do the writing he said he wanted to. But he never does any.'

That was a sore point, Caroline realised, the cause of some of Fenella's dissatisfaction with Harry.

'Are you really sure he never does any?' she asked. 'If he knows you're expecting him to do the "serious" writing you talked about this evening, and he's just dashing off things he thinks you'd despise, perhaps he'd keep it secret.'

Fenella shook her head. 'Look, if you were a writer, would you worry much what I thought of your stuff? Well, Harry doesn't either. He knows I haven't any judgment. And he knows it wasn't I who wanted him to do the serious writing. It was he who wanted it. I'd be quite happy if he just wrote something, anything.'

72

'He probably needs time,' Caroline said. 'I shouldn't worry too much about it.'

'Oh, I don't, really.' Fenella shrugged it off. 'It's the money I worry about. For instance, where did he get the money to buy this house?'

Caroline had wondered about that herself. 'What did you have to give for it?' she asked.

'The price was five thousand. We've a big mortgage on it, though, so we only had to put down the deposit, which was about twelve hundred.'

'Which Harry produced?'

'Yes, and the money to do it up and furnish it, which came to quite a lot more. He said he had it in a savings account that he hadn't told me about before, because he wanted it to be a big surprise for me. Harry with a savings account—can you imagine it?'

Caroline reached for an ash-tray and crushed out her cigarette. 'You know, it sounds to me as if there's a quite simple explanation for all this,' she said. 'It's just that Harry's far more secretive about money than you've realised. He did have a savings account which he didn't tell you about till he wanted to use the money in it, and now he's probably got another account besides your joint one, which he likes to feel you don't know all about either.'

Fenella shook her head again. 'I thought of that myself, but I don't believe it.'

'Why not?'

'There'd still be the problem of where the money was coming from.'

'Perhaps he gambles a bit. Doesn't he ever bet on horses, or dogs, or anything?'

'Sometimes, but when he does he gets excited and talks a lot about it,' Fenella said. 'He always spends it straight away too, generally on a present for me. He'd never dream of keeping it secret.'

'Then tell me what it is you really believe about him.' Caroline had begun to feel sure that at the back of her mind Fenella had already found a solution to the problem that was haunting her and that she was stubbornly determined not to consider any other.

Fenella only gave a sigh and did not answer.

After a moment, with impatience creeping into her voice, Caroline said, 'Well, tell me about the man who came asking questions.'

'He was an odd little man who arrived one morning while Harry was out doing the shopping,' Fenella answered. 'A jerky, twitchy, foxy-faced little man. He began by asking about a room here. I didn't take to him at all, so I started saying we were full up, but somehow he got into the sitting-room and sat down and started talking about this and that, and in a way he was quite amusing and I started laughing, and it was some time before I realised he was asking me questions about everybody, Harry and Mr. Sherwin and Mrs. Dewhurst.'

'And Jan Pullen?'

'Yes,' Fenella admitted reluctantly, 'about him too.'

'I suppose you've heard about the man he's had around, also asking questions,' Caroline said.

'Who, Jan?'

'Yes, he told Harry about him this afternoon, just before the accident. A quite different-looking man.'

Fenella smoothed her skirt down and folded her fidgeting hands. She said musingly, 'I haven't seen Jan for days.'

'The point is, this man's questions weren't specially about Harry either. So there's no reason why you should jump to the conclusion it's only Harry they're interested in.'

'I know, but still it means there's something peculiar about somebody here. Which is what Harry keeps saying, isn't it? He says Mr. Sherwin burnt his shop down to collect the insurance, and he says Mrs. Dewhurst murdered her husband, and even if you know he doesn't mean it, he means *something*—I know he does. You heard him this evening talking about how much he knows about certain people, and how he's got it all written down somewhere . . .'

Her voice faded, as if, when she came to put it into words, she could not really believe in the conclusion at which she had nearly arrived.

But at last Caroline understood what was

haunting her.

'Fenella, I believe you've got it into your head he's *blackmailing* somebody!'

Fenella sprang to her feet, her cheeks blazing.

'All right, it's funny!' she cried. 'Funny as hell! So funny you could almost die laughing about it. But you try living with it on your mind and see what that does to you.'

'I'm not laughing,' Caroline said soberly. 'I was just—oh, taken by surprise. It seems so . . .' She spread her hands in a gesture of helplessness.

'So fantastic, so impossible! I know, I know, I've been through all that! But if you don't believe me, you won't be able to help me—and I think I'm going mad!'

Fenella ran out of the room, slamming the door behind her.

Caroline dropped her head into her hands and shut her eyes. She remained like that for some minutes, then she got up and started to undress. Her head was aching and if she made an incautious movement, all her bruises hurt. She kept thinking of everything that she knew about Harry, which was very little and was wholly dominated by what he had done that afternoon, so that at first it seemed easy to convince herself that there couldn't be a shred of justification for Fenella's fears. Yet when she might have started thinking about something else, she found herself going over the same ground again and again, and gradually, as the time passed, found her first conviction growing less and less clear and positive.

Harry was really such a violent little man, and so full of jealousy, suspicion and strangeness that it was hard to be sure of anything about him. He didn't want you to be sure. He wanted you to be puzzled and mixed up. It gave him a feeling of power. And if he wanted power of that kind, mightn't he want it too in other, more dangerous forms? Was that so incredible?

By the time that Caroline had started asking herself that question and finding it not particularly bizarre, she was in bed and, in spite of her tiredness, had become painfully wakeful. She knew that she had a bad night coming. In the distance the noise of hammering from Jan Pullen's garage was more persistent than usual and it seemed to be thudding directly on her nerves, keeping time maddeningly with the throbbing in her temples, or else getting sickeningly, deliberately out of time. Obviously she was in no state to think anything out. The smallest problem would turn into a nightmare. Switching on the light by the bed, she reached for a book.

But her worries were not so easily defeated. She had to fight a desperate battle with the print to stop it continually swimming away into a foggy blur. Several times she turned a number of pages without having taken in a single thing that she had read. She swallowed some aspirin, but the headache grew no better.

It was the old feeling of responsibility for Fenella that was the trouble, a feeling that she had foresworn a dozen times, since it seemed to do nothing for either of them, yet which had never quite faded. But you couldn't help the girl. From the time when she had grown out of childhood into an aloof, highly strung adolescence which, Caroline thought, had really persisted ever since, there had been nothing you could do for her but leave her alone. Nothing, at least, that Caroline knew how to do.

Anyway, she mused, frowning at the undulating print on the page before her, who was she to offer help to anyone? Had she made such a fine thing of her life? To have achieved the great success of being told that they did not know what to do without her in the office, and to realise that that was probably about all that she was ever going to achieve, did that qualify her for offering advice on the mysteries of marriage?

She gave her advice freely enough in the office, even when it wasn't asked for. It was part of her public character. Miss Dyer going forth on the war-path, squaring her jaw and fiercely pushing up her sleeves as she went, as if she might need her fists in the argument, was one of the office jokes. A joke she had half-consciously fostered, but distinctly a joke.

Or was that her mistake? Was it the sober and discouraging truth that that rather domineering person, who always knew her own mind and who took immediate steps that others should know it too, and for whom, if she had ever taken her seriously, she would have had no great liking, was what she really was?

That was what Fenella had always taken for granted. She had no knowledge of, or at least no interest in, the other side of her sister's nature, the side that had had to have that little flat in Ealing to come alive in. By which, for once, Fenella perhaps showed sense, since that other side of Caroline had never been of much use to anyone that she could remember, or not for a long, long time. It was just a sort of self-indulgence.

So the thing to do now was to ignore it. Be what Fenella expected and wanted. Provide her with some hard and fast opinion about Harry, if only so that she could react against it with a good conscience. Only how could one think about something like that, or about anything at all, while that damned hammering was going on? On and on, on and on, until suddenly it was broad daylight and Caroline found herself rubbing her eyes and realising that she must have been asleep for some hours and that the hammering she could hear now was someone knocking at her door.

It was Mrs. Freely, one of the women from the village who came to help Fenella with the cleaning, and who now had Caroline's breakfast on a tray. She was full of sympathy about the accident, shaking her head, clicking her tongue, saying you sometimes wondered, didn't you, when you went out in the morning if you'd ever get home alive again, and if anyone asked, she wouldn't mind betting she could tell them who'd been driving the van.

Caroline felt that she was expected to ask whom Mrs. Freely had in mind, but when she did so Mrs. Freely only said she didn't hold with talking, and backing out of the door, advised Caroline to have a good lie in, because she could believe Mrs. Freely, she wasn't missing anything. This naturally, had the effect of making Caroline feel that she had better get up as quickly as possible to find out just what it was that she was missing.

But when she presently went downstairs, she at first noticed nothing wrong. Harry, Fenella, Mrs. Dewhurst and Mr. Sherwin were still sitting round the breakfast table, as if they felt too tired, too disorganised to start the normal activities of the day and had dropped into an idle discussion. At the moment when Caroline came in they were all silent, and she was just beginning to say that she would like another cup of coffee when Jan Pullen went by outside the window.

With her nerves still raw from the noise in the night, her impulse was to go straight out to meet him and tell him in plain terms how she was feeling about him, but Harry quickly thrust past her and went to the front door. Caroline again started to say that she would like some coffee, but Fenella took no notice of her. She only sat there, intently listening as Harry called out a greeting to Jan. They were all listening, she realised, with just a little too much tension for comfort.

After a minute or two Harry brought Jan into the dining-room. Harry's manner was casual and quite friendly as he pulled a chair forward for Jan, offered him coffee, which he refused, then a cigarette, which Jan reached for with one of his big, battered, mechanic's hands, then lit with a gold lighter that he brought out of a pocket in his stained overalls.

While he and Harry discussed the car which Jan had towed to his garage yesterday, once the police had allowed it to be moved, he fiddled with the lighter, flicking it on and off without thinking.

'I honestly think you'd be wise to dump the thing on the scrapheap, Harry,' he said, 'unless you want to spend a fortune. I haven't really looked into it yet, but my impression is you should take the insurance and forget the thing.'

'I see,' Harry said. 'That's that, then.' He tugged at his chin. 'But can't I get something for the wreck?'

'Oh, I'll take it off your hands, if you like,' Jan said. 'I might be able to put it into some sort of shape, given time. If not, I can always use the spare parts. When I've looked into things more carefully, I'll give you a price.'

'All right,' Harry said. But he sounded dubious. He had started to frown.

'Don't take my word for it,' Jan said, seeing it. 'You can get on to the people in Rudbourne.' Suddenly he became aware of Caroline, staring at the lighter in his hand, and slipped it back into a pocket. 'I'm glad you don't seem to have suffered too seriously, Miss Dyer.'

He had not looked once at Fenella since he had come into the room, though she was watching him steadily, with what, Caroline supposed, was meant to be an expressionless face.

Harry answered for Caroline. 'Oh, she feels fine. A nice little accident was just what she needed to set her up.'

Jan stood up. 'Well, let me know what you want me to do, Harry. Meanwhile I'll look into things more thoroughly.'

Then, as if he had decided beforehand that he would allow himself one glance, and one glance only, at Fenella, he took it, like snatching up a glass of potent spirit and pouring it straight down his throat. Then he went out.

There was silence again in the room after he had gone. Everyone there had seen what was in that look. They could not have missed it.

Harry went back to his place at the table. There was a calm, crooked smile on his face. His blue eyes lingered absently for a moment on Fenella's.

'How odd to run into that business again,' he observed thoughtfully. 'How awfully odd.'

Fenella's voice shot up wildly. 'What do you mean, Harry?'

'The old familiar racket,' he said.

Mrs. Dewhurst gave a nervous giggle. 'Oh, a racket!' she said, as if she were delighted to hear that that was all it was. 'I thought—I was afraid—' She put a hand to her mouth and subsided.

Harry went on, 'Haven't you got on to it yet? It's funny, his trying it on me, of all people. I once reported the trial of a man who'd been getting away with it for years. Remember, Fenella? It was just about the first time we met.'

Her knife dropped on to her plate with a clatter. There was no beauty in her face at that moment. It was long and white and ugly with pain.

'For some reason the case fascinated me,' Harry said, 'so I did a good deal of investigating and found out a lot about the set-up. The man used to appear on the scene of an accident and buy up the damaged car very cheap, saying he wanted it for the spare parts. Then he'd steal a car of the same make and same year, transfer the registration, etc., from the old one, then sell the stolen car as the smashed-up one on which he'd done a brilliant job of repairs. It all looked very nice and legal, and as a matter of fact, the police had a devil of a job proving the thing against him. He was very smooth and plausible, with a public school accent and a good car and a smart blonde wife who helped around the place. At least, the neighbours thought she was his wife till a quite different one turned up at the trial, a terrific tough creature who sat and gloated over his downfall. I believe he got five years.'

Fenella sprang to her feet. She pounded the table with one of the hands that looked so helpless and were really so strong.

'Why do you have to lie, and lie, and lie?' she cried. 'You know there isn't a word of truth in all that.'

Harry cocked a sardonic eyebrow at her. 'Darling, I can dig up the clippings in a few minutes, if you'd like to see them.'

'But that Jan—that he's doing that—you *know* it's a lie!'

'I wonder why you're so sure.'

At the other end of the table Mr. Sherwin suddenly stood up. Caroline thought that he was going to say something to make Harry stop his jealous baiting of Fenella. For that was all it was, Caroline was sure. He was taking his revenge for the look that Jan Pullen had given her.

But to Caroline's surprise, Mr. Sherwin spoke to her.

'I think a change of atmosphere might do you good, Miss Dyer,' he said. 'How would you like to come into Rudbourne with me this morning? I'd like to show you the remains of my bookshop.'

CHAPTER SEVEN

'There are times,' Mr. Sherwin said some minutes later, as he and Caroline walked to the garage, 'when a husband and wife should be left to themselves, even when they take paying guests.'

'Oh, I agree!' Caroline said with feeling.

'And there are times when a person who's supposed to be recuperating from an illness, with an odd accident thrown in to complicate matters, ought not to have to take too much of other people's emotional stresses. Or so I thought, looking at you just now.'

She laughed. 'It's exactly how I was feeling, Mr. Sherwin. Convalescents are notoriously selfish.'

'Of course, they may not actually have wanted us to leave.' He pushed open the garage doors, which no one ever bothered to lock. 'Lyddon loves playing to an audience. I just took the view that it would be better for them if we did leave, and much, much better for you.'

'And I'm very grateful. I was just thinking I'd have to go for a long walk.'

'Hardly a nice morning for that.'

It was not. There was a cold mist on the hills, not very dense, but clammy and penetrating. Caroline shivered as she waited for Mr. Sherwin to unlock his car, and turning up the collar of her blue tweed coat, from which she had just brushed the mud-stains, wished that she had brought a scarf to tie over her hair. The mist would flatten out every scrap of wave still left in it.

'And I doubt if you're up to a long walk yet,' he said, opening a door of the car for her to get in. 'You know, what I think I'd do as soon as possible, if I were you, Miss Dyer, is get on a plane and go to a nice Greek island.'

'How I wish I'd thought of that in time!' she said with a laugh.

'Is it too late for it now?'

'I'm afraid I've a job where I don't want to let them forget my existence.'

'I'm sure there's no danger of that. You're probably the rock on which the whole show is founded.'

'Me—a rock? I've never felt less like one. Oh, look—' The front door had just opened and Mrs. Dewhurst came out. 'She seems to think she ought to go for a walk too.'

Mrs. Dewhurst saw them and came hurrying towards the car. She had a scarf over her head and a plastic cover over the scarf and a plastic cape over her coat, so that she looked all wrapped up in whiteness, as the hills were in mist.

Winding down the window beside him, Mr. Sherwin asked, 'Can I give you a lift anywhere, Mrs. Dewhurst?'

'Oh no, thank you. I'm just going for my little stroll,' she said. 'One must have exercise. Otherwise I put on weight so terribly. I'm not really used to sitting and doing nothing, I'm usually very active, only now, of course, I have to be careful. But that isn't what I wanted to say. I wanted to ask you if you get as upset as I do by that awful hammering in the night. Last night I hardly slept at all. I know that was partly because of all the excitement yesterday, but the hammering was really the last straw.'

Mr. Sherwin looked questioningly at Caroline. 'Did it worry you too? I slept like a log myself.'

Before Caroline could answer, Mrs. Dewhurst hurried on. 'I'm wondering if perhaps we oughtn't to protest about it, only I do so hate making trouble. But would it be unreasonable, do you think, to suggest to the young man he shouldn't go on after, say, half past ten? Or eleven? He seems a very pleasant young man and I expect he doesn't realise how the sound carries.'

'Then you don't agree with Lyddon that he's a car-thief?' Mr. Sherwin said.

Mrs. Dewhurst tittered uneasily. 'Oh, Mr. Sherwin!'

'That hammering of his could be when he's making over the stolen cars. But I'll see what I can do,' he promised. 'I rather like the idea of asking a car-thief not to ply his trade after ten-thirty. I wonder how he'd take it.'

Her face blanched. 'You don't mean you think Mr. Lyddon was *serious*? Oh no, he's almost never serious.'

'Well, if you're sure you don't want a lift . . .' He started the car.

Mrs. Dewhurst stood still where she was, staring after it, a blue-white bundle of a woman in her plastic wrappings, soon swallowed up by the mist. Blue-white, Caroline suddenly thought, because the coat under the semi-transparent cape was blue. Almost the same blue as her own. And they both had dark hair too. Did that make sense of Mrs. Dewhurst's startling question about whether Caroline had been wearing her blue coat at the time of the accident?

Glancing at her sideways, Mr. Sherwin said, 'You're looking a little shocked, Miss Dyer. Do you think I was unkind to her?'

'You were, rather,' she answered.

'It's how she affects me,' he said. 'She seems born to be baited.'

'But actually I was thinking . . .' She paused, realising that she did not want to talk about the blue coats and Mrs. Dewhurst's question. Not when they had already had more than enough melodrama from Harry about the accident. 'I wonder what's the matter with her,' she said.

'She's just a poor, stupid woman who can't stand up for herself,' he answered. 'It brings out the brute in all of us.'

'No, I meant when she said she had to be careful . . . But if she's ill, it explains how she lives, doesn't it?'

'She doesn't look ill.'

'Heart cases often don't.'

'If she's a heart case, she ought to be warned about her passion for your brother-in-law's cooking.' He glanced at her again. 'What's really worrying you?'

She shook her head. 'Nothing special. But suppose . . .' Again she changed what she had nearly said. 'Suppose Jan Pullen really is a car-thief.'

'So Lyddon's at last convinced somebody.'

'No.' Then with exasperation she went on, 'No, of course he hasn't. Yet somehow he produces the feeling in one that at least some of what he says must be true. One tries to resist it, but it starts to grow on one.'

'Well, it would be surprising, with his intelligence, if he didn't hit the nail on the head just occasionally.'

'Only when he does, no one's going to believe him.'

'So you're wondering if you oughtn't to try. Perhaps it'll come with practice, as it did with the White Queen.'

'You don't much like him, do you?'

He drove for a moment in silence, then he said, 'I'd find it interesting to know how far you've got in believing that I burnt my shop down to collect the insurance.'

Caroline's cheeks flamed. 'Oh, please—'

He laughed. 'Don't worry, he says it to everyone, and if he didn't someone else would say it. I hope to live it down in time. But I've been thinking recently that even his cooking doesn't quite compensate me for having to put up with him.'

They had reached the chalk cutting and started downwards into the valley beyond. The mist was thinner on this side of the downs and was brightened by a faint iridescence of sunshine.

He went on, 'I think it's going to be a fine day after all. By the way, about going to the shop now, you haven't got to come and look at it if it doesn't interest you. I'm going there because I've got an appointment with the builders at eleven, but I only suggested you should come because it was the first thing that came into my head when I suddenly decided we ought to remove ourselves.'

'I'd like to see it,' Caroline said, 'if I shan't

be in the way.'

'Only there's nothing much to see,' he said. 'Just the basement. The stuff there wasn't damaged much, except at one end, where the water got through. But the house has gone. They've finished the demolition and the rebuilding hasn't started yet.'

'When do you think you'll be able to open it up again?'

'I'm not sure I mean to open it up again.'

'I'd have thought you'd be longing to,' she said. 'I thought it meant a great deal to you.'

'It isn't as simple as that.' They were passing the garage, but evidently he had forgotten that he had promised to convey Mrs. Dewhurst's complaint to Jan Pullen. 'No,' he said, 'you'll see, it isn't simple at all.'

In Rudbourne he parked the car in the church square, then led Caroline into a narrow close of old houses. Some of them were half-timbered, some were of a dim red brick with sash windows. None of them had been intended as shops in the first place, but most of them now had small shop windows carved as discreetly as possible into their aged walls. There were two antique shops, a confectioner, a bootmaker, a milliner, a shop that sold nothing but cheeses. There was a sedately uncommercial air of quiet about the place, preserved by a row of posts across the entrance to the close, which kept out the traffic.

The remains of the bookshop were

concealed by a wooden hoarding that spanned a gap between the milliner's and the cheese shop. Only some scaffolding showed above the hoarding, supporting the walls of the houses on each side. There were still fireplaces to be seen on the walls, one of them with a much blackened but delicately carved marble mantelpiece. It looked sad and foolish up there, its charming intimacy exposed, like a slightly lunatic old lady, talking to herself in public.

'Sure you want to come in?' the bookseller asked, stopping in front of a door in the hoarding.

'Yes, please,' Caroline said.

He unlocked the padlock on the door.

'The odd thing is, I'm already beginning to forget what it used to be like.' Pushing open the door, he went through it, unlocked a gate in some area railings just inside, and led the way down some steps to the basement entrance.

The basement was a gloomy place with small windows below ground level and no electricity now to light it up. The room at the front was the one that the water had got into. It was empty, with a strong smell of mould in it and with grey, furry patches of mildew on the walls.

The books that had been saved were in a smaller room at the back of the house, packed into bookcases and stacked on the floor. They were a tattered-looking collection, some still in fairly new dust-jackets, some in worn leather bindings, some without bindings at all. The smell of mould had seeped in from the other room and there was dust everywhere.

'The irony of things,' Mr. Sherwin said as he tumbled some books off a chair, blew some dust off it and pushed it towards Caroline. 'There's nothing of any value here. All the good stuff was upstairs.'

'But isn't any of this any use?' she asked as she sat down. 'There's such a lot of it.'

'All junk,' he answered. 'I've been going through it slowly in hope—or really just to have something to do, while I try to make up my mind about the future. I thought if I found anything of real interest, it might make me feel like starting again.'

'Don't you know what's here? Haven't you any records?'

'They were upstairs too,' he said. 'But they wouldn't have told me much about this lot. My father and my grandfather used this as the dump. From time to time, to make room, they'd send some of it off to a cheap sale, but mostly it just piled up. So there's just a chance, or so I tell myself, that some things were put here that shouldn't have been. But actually it isn't very likely. They both knew their trade a great deal better than I do.'

'I didn't realise it had been in your family for such a long time,' she said. 'Doesn't that make you feel you've got to get it going again?'

'Is that what you think I ought to feel?'

She smiled uncertainly. 'I think I might. I don't know.'

He went on, 'My great-grandfather started it. That's to say, he started the collection and sometimes sold a few things to buy others. A very gentlemanly business. Then my grandfather extended it and really built up our reputation, but still it was only collectors' items. He'd customers all over the world, but there was no sign of a shop-window or a name over the door. It was my father who turned it into a shop in the ordinary sense, but still it was the sale of rare books that kept it going. An ordinary second-hand bookshop in a town like Rudbourne wouldn't have been very profitable. Then I took over.' He gestured at the rubble of books at his feet. 'And this is all that's left.'

'And to start a new collection, would that take too long?' Caroline asked.

'And too much determination, too much enthusiasm.'

She looked up at him curiously as he stood before her in the dim, dusty room. His back was towards the small window, so that really she could see nothing of him but his thin, stooping outline. She could not see any of the forcefulness that she had seen in him the evening before. It seemed obscured by the dimness and dustiness.

'I thought till now that you had all the enthusiasm you needed,' she said. 'I didn't understand the problem.'

He picked up a battered volume from the top of a heap and fluttered the pages.

'It was of fairly recent birth, such enthusiasm as I had. When I was a boy, the one lasting dream I had was of getting out. I'd change my mind about what I wanted to get out into—sometimes it was farming in Australia, and sometimes I thought I'd make a wonderful medical missionary in Africa, and sometimes I thought I'd like to be a scientist of some sort and explore the Arctic—just anything, in fact, where there weren't a lot of books. And then the war came along and I had to get out into the army, and then I started to dream about books.' He gave a deprecatory laugh. 'Not books to read, you know. Just books to look at and handle and smell. So here I am.'

'You mean, regretting it?'

'The truth is, I don't know what I mean. If there hadn't been this holocaust . . . No, I don't know. But I could use the insurance money to get started on something new, and it's now or never. But what would our friend Harry Lyddon have to say to that?'

'Harry?' Caroline said with a start. 'What's he got to do with it? . . . Oh, I see! No, that's too ridiculous. You can't mean you think you've got to start again just to show people you didn't burn the place down on purpose.'

'Sometimes it seems to me the only good reason,' he said.

'I should say the only thing that matters is, do you want to and can you?'

'Is that how you run your own affairs? Don't you worry about what other people think of you?'

'Of course I do. Some people. Not Harry.'

'Why not Harry?'

'For one thing, because I don't know how one ever finds out what he's honestly thinking.'

He tossed the book that he had been holding back on to its pile.

'All I know,' he said, 'is that the story that I burnt the place down for the sake of the insurance is the kind that could follow me a long way and for a long time, and that I find I mind the thought of it much more than perhaps I should.'

'Then you must be much angrier with Harry than you've admitted.'

'No, not really. It's only at odd moments that it occurs to me to take him seriously. I'm really very sorry for him—and still more for his wife. But I don't find them a very persuasive argument for starting a new life. I don't think he'll ever do any of that writing they both talk about, and she's quite deeply disappointed about that, and he's bored—bored and looking for trouble, with all that frenzied energy of his going to waste. However, I don't know why we keep talking so much about him. Let's get out of here. Let's go and have some coffee.'

They climbed the area steps again, to find that while they had been in the basement the mist had lifted and the sky was deepening blue. It felt good to be out of the mildew-tainted air. They had coffee in one of the little houses at the far end of the close, in a warm bright room that smelt of coffee and fresh baking.

Over their coffee, Mr. Sherwin told Caroline some more of the history of the bookshop. He told her stories of exciting finds, of book thieves, of curious customers. It was long past eleven o'clock when he remembered his appointment with the builder.

'I don't suppose he'll have waited,' he said ruefully, 'but I suppose I ought to go and see. But the question is, how do you get home? Can you wait somewhere? As soon as I'm through with him I could pick you up and drive you back.'

'Aren't there any buses to Dexter Abbas?' Caroline asked.

'Yes, but I don't know when they go and they only go to the village. It's quite a walk after that.'

'It'll probably do me good,' she said.

However, when they went out again into the close and parted outside the door in the hoarding, she did not go straight back to Dexter Abbas, although he had told her where to find the bus station. Instead, she went

97

looking for a hairdresser, had her hair done and afterwards had lunch in a café in the main street. It was a dreary place, decorated with dusty plastic plants in plastic pots, but there was a sense of luxury simply in being out on her own again. A sign of age, no doubt, certainly a sign of settled spinsterhood, but there it was. She enjoyed the roast beef that had been re-warmed in some lumpy brown gravy, the damp potatoes and the pale liquid with milky skins floating on the top, described as coffee, more than she could possibly have enjoyed one of Harry's best efforts.

She would have liked to put off her return to the guesthouse for some hours, for the longer that Harry and Fenella were left to themselves, the better chance there was of the atmosphere having simmered down to normal by the time she arrived. And it would have been pleasant to stroll in the sunshine, to do a little unnecessary shopping, perhaps to go to a cinema. But unfortunately, when she had paid her bill and walked out into the sparkling afternoon, she found that she had only an intense longing to lie down. Nothing else had any attractions whatever. Abruptly her energy had run out. She felt dizzy and a little sick. The thought of the journey by bus and the walk from the village was quite horrifying.

Luckily there was a taxi-rank in the first side-street that she came to. Plunging into the first taxi, she put her feet up and shut her eyes.

Most of the way to Dexter Abbas the driver chatted to her in a Dorset accent so broad that she could hardly follow him, but she did not have to answer and gradually her dizziness passed. Instead, a wild impatience possessed her. When was she going to be well again, free of the risk of these sudden collapses? When would she be able to stand on her own feet, to go back to work? She had been nearly there and then that damned accident had had to happen, and now here she was, feeling almost as weak as when she had first arrived. She thought with fury of the drunken van-driver.

As she did so, she saw the van itself. It was standing at Jan Pullen's pumps, and Jan was there, talking to the driver. Caroline cried out to her driver to stop. He did not understand her in time but he had slowed down for the turning into the narrow road that led up to the chalk cutting, and as the van came out of the garage and passed within a foot of the taxi, Caroline and the driver looked straight at one another.

The man smiled. It seemed a pleased smile, as if he were surprised, but pleasantly, to find a woman staring so intently at him. But then the recognition on Caroline's face must have told him who she was, and where they had met before, for his own face changed. The grin became a grimace of frenzied fear. He shouted something at her and shook his fist, then drove off as if the whole police-force was after him.

CHAPTER EIGHT

The taxi-driver, after saying what he thought, was going to drive on.

'No, I want to get out!' Caroline cried excitedly. 'Wait a minute!'

'Here, miss? But you said—'

'I know, I've changed my mind.' She pushed open the door of the taxi, jumped out and handed the man a pound note.

Jan Pullen, beside his pumps, stood watching her, his hands in the pockets of his overalls.

The driver counted her change into her hand with maddening slowness.

'You want me to wait, did you say, miss?'

'No, I just meant, put me down here,' she said.

'I can wait, if you want me to.'

'No, thank you. I'm not sure how long I'll be.'

'I don't mind waiting.'

'Thank you, it's quite all right.'

She dropped the change into her bag and snapped it shut.

As she walked towards the young man, who made no move to come towards her, she unconsciously started trying to push up the sleeves of her coat, as if she were preparing for battle. Her fatigue had vanished. She had forgotten that she felt ill.

'So you do know that man,' she said.

Jan Pullen returned her stare woodenly. His dark face looked surly and tired.

'What man?' he asked.

'That man in the van.'

'Jack Dawson? Runs a small carrier's business. What's he done?'

'Mr. Pullen, you know what he's done,' she said. 'He drove Harry's car off the road and nearly killed us.'

He arched his thick, black eyebrows. 'Jack Dawson?'

'Yes, Jack Dawson, if that's his name.'

'No, Miss Dyer.' He shook his head. 'It wasn't the same van.'

Caroline clenched her fists. 'Doesn't anyone around here ever speak the truth? I *saw* him, Mr. Pullen. It's the same van, the same man, and you know it. You've known it all along.'

'I'm sorry, you're mistaken. There are dozens of vans like that on the road. I didn't notice anything special about the one that came in here yesterday, but I know it wasn't Jack Dawson's.'

She went a step nearer to him. Her anger brought a brighter colour into her cheeks than had been there since the beginning of her illness.

'Listen, he saw me, he recognised me, he shook his fist at me. Didn't you see that? There's no point in pretending he's a different man.'

He began to say something, checked himself and answered indifferently, 'All right, I do know him. And now what?'

'First tell me why you said you didn't know him.'

'My affair, isn't it?'

'And mine. And Harry's.'

'I don't really think it is.'

'And what about the police? Didn't you tell Sergeant Rutter you didn't know the man?'

'Yes, I did.'

'Why?'

He took his time before he answered, bringing cigarettes out of his pocket, holding them out to Caroline and, when she refused, putting one in his mouth and lighting it with his gold lighter.

At last he replied, 'Harry was behaving like a lunatic, wasn't he? Well, you don't always tell a lunatic the truth. You tell him what it's safest and best for him to know.'

'Sergeant Rutter isn't a lunatic.'

He shrugged his shoulders. 'The police will get on to Jack soon enough without my help. But by then Harry may have calmed down and be ready to tell them a saner version of what happened.'

'I can tell them a sane version now.'

'You want vengeance, do you? I thought better of you.'

'I want to keep a dangerous man off the

road.'

'Without knowing anything about him? Without knowing what you might be doing to him?'

'I know what he may be doing this moment to someone else, and it ought to be stopped.' She turned back towards the road. 'I'm going to the police.'

Jan Pullen let her go a few steps, then he came after her. 'I think we ought to talk this over.'

'All right,' she said, 'talk. I'm ready to listen.'

'Come inside, then.'

'Is there so much to say?'

'You never know till you get started.'

She tried not to show that what she had intended from the first was to get into his garage, and answered indifferently, 'Very well.' But as they went in, she looked round eagerly.

The wreck of Harry's car was in a corner. Most of its glass was smashed and there was an enormous dent in the side. It was the side on which she had been sitting. If it had been a little farther back, she would not have been there now, looking at it. It was a reminder that there had been nothing lunatic about Harry when the accident happened. It was Jack Dawson who was the lunatic, and that wasn't only a manner of speaking. After what had just happened in the lane, she felt sure that the man was not sane.

'Do you run this place all by yourself?' she

asked curiously.

'At the moment I do,' the young man said. 'I'd a boy helping till last week, but he was always getting under my feet, so I decided I was better off without him. Come in here, will you?'

He opened a door at the back of the garage.

The door led into a small room that contained a desk, a telephone, a wooden chair, a calendar on the wall, some ledgers on a shelf and an electric radiator, which Jan Pullen switched on before propping himself against the doorpost. Caroline was disappointed. The room could not have told her less about him. Certainly it was not the place where he did his mysterious hammering in the night. Neither had there been anything in the garage itself to suggest that he did it there.

She sat down on the one wooden chair. 'Well?' she said.

He answered quickly this time, 'All right, I may have been wrong yesterday to say I didn't know Jack. Probably I was. I'm still not quite sure about it, but I may have been. But there are times—this is what I wanted to tell you about—there are times when a man's got to be given a chance, and if ever you've met a man who needs a chance, it's Jack Dawson.'

'A chance to knock some more people off the road?' Caroline suggested. 'To make a better job of it next time?'

'Listen, for God's sake!' he said. 'Until three

months ago Jack was as sober and quiet as any man alive. Then his wife left him. Suddenly went off with another man. No warning beforehand. He hadn't even been suspicious of her till then. He thought they were a nice happy family, allowing for the fact that they live in a row of awful cottages near here that haven't any drainage, and have only one pump to the lot, and are all falling apart with dry rot. It's a real rural slum. You might go along and look at it. And there are three young children . . . No, wait a moment!' He raised a hand to stop Caroline interrupting. 'Don't say that doesn't make any difference. He's got to look after the kids and somehow keep things going, hasn't he? The neighbours aren't much use. The respectable ones turn up their noses at the ones who live in the slum, and most of the others are a good deal worse than Jack. And the van's his livelihood.'

His voice had become eager and persuasive. His face had lost its surliness and become appealing.

Caroline turned her head away, looking out of the window.

Because she was thinking over what he had been saying, it took her a moment to notice that she was looking at something rather interesting. It was a small barn that had been hidden from the road by the taller garage.

Studying this building thoughtfully, she said, 'Isn't it possible that stopping his driving before something really awful happens is the best thing that could happen to him?'

'That's an easy thing to say,' Jan answered. 'You aren't the one with the kids.'

'No, I'm just the one who was lucky to get off with only a few bruises.'

She saw that the barn was an old one, but it had a new, stout door, fastened with a padlock. Near the door there was a small, cobwebby window. The grime on the glass and the cobwebs alone would have made it difcult enough to see through it, but besides these there was a curtain of some sort inside. It looked like a piece of sacking that had been nailed to the frame. Whatever Jan Pullen did in the barn, it seemed he wanted complete privacy for it.

'Oh, I know Jack's a menace at present,' he was saying. 'But he's really a decent sort of chap, and he's going through such hell.'

'Did you realise he was drunk yesterday when you filled his tank up?' Caroline asked.

'Drunk? No,' he said. 'That's to say, it didn't strike me he was any drunker than a lot of people who drop in here for petrol on their way home from a party in one of the bigger houses hereabouts. Can you imagine their faces if I refused to fill up their tanks?'

'It wasn't your filling up his tank I was thinking about,' she said.' It was your real reason for telling the police you didn't know him.'

'I've just been trying to tell you that,' he said.

'I wonder if you have.'

They looked at one another silently for a moment. There was dismay on his face, as if he were regretting the approach that he had made to her.

'D'you know, I'd got you all wrong,' he said. 'I thought I could make you listen.'

'I have listened, haven't I? But I'm still puzzled at what you did. I'm puzzled by lots of things about you.'

'Well, don't let that prejudice you against Jack. Think what it felt like to hear Harry shouting at me on the phone that Jack had deliberately tried to kill him and that I'd tried to help. Did you hear him?'

'I heard some of it.'

'And remember I wasn't even sure there'd been an accident at all. You can never be sure with Harry. For some reason he'd got in a rage with me when I told him about the man who'd been here asking questions. I didn't know what the rage was all about, but I saw it burning him up, and when he telephoned with his story about the accident, I actually thought it might be just some complicated way of getting back at me. I was all wrong, of course, but I wasn't sure of that till the police turned up. Even then, I didn't want Jack offered up as a sacrifice to whatever Harry's got against me.'

If he didn't know what Harry had against

him, Caroline thought, or even if he merely believed that she didn't know, he must be stupider than he seemed.

'Harry told us,' she said, 'that it didn't occur to him that the van-driver was anything but a drunk until you denied knowing him and his being drunk when you saw him.'

'Then it's his story against mine—take your pick.'

'Unless there's a third story.'

'Oh, of course, there's Jack's own story,' he said. 'Why don't you go and talk to him and find out for yourself that he isn't a murdering fiend?'

It had not been the van-driver's story that she had meant, but a different story that Jan might perhaps have told her, if he had wanted to.

'I think I shall probably do that,' she said, and stood up.

'That's really all I'm asking.' He moved from the doorway to let her come out. 'I'd just like to be sure that you know all the facts before you rush to the police to tell them you've seen Jack again. Now I'll drive you up to the house, if you don't mind being seen in this thing.' He pointed at his own dilapidated car.

Relieved that she had not got to face the walk up the hill, she got in and he drove her as far as the stone gate-posts, but left her to walk up the drive alone.

As she approached the house, she began to wonder what she would find when she reached it. Harry and Fenella still quarrelling? Refusing to speak to each other? Agreed on divorce? Or reconciled and somewhat the happier for having been able to have their row in peace?

Whichever it might be, Caroline did not want to risk walking into the middle of an emotional crisis, so as soon as she opened the door, she called out, 'Fenella, I'm back!'

The kitchen door opened and Harry came prancing out.

He had on the striped butcher's apron that he always wore for cooking and was holding a wicked-looking kitchen knife in his hand. A smell of garlic and simmering wine followed him. His blue eyes were bright and smiling.

'By yourself?' he said. 'What's happened to Sherwin?'

'Oh, we separated hours ago,' she answered. 'He had business with the builder.'

'Then how did you get home?'

'A taxi.' She had decided not to mention yet that she had stopped at the garage and in fact had finished the journey in Jan Pullen's car.

'Extravagant!' Harry said. 'If you'd rung up, I'd have fetched you . . . No, of course, I couldn't, I haven't got a car. I hope Sherwin gets back soon because we're counting on being able to use his. We're all going out this evening.'

'All?' Caroline said in alarm. 'I'm sorry, Harry, I'm feeling just about dead.'

'Well, go and have a good rest then and perhaps you'll be all right by the evening. We want everyone to come and even Mrs. Dewhurst says she will. It's a celebration.'

'We seem to be doing a lot of celebrating at the moment,' Caroline said as she started up the stairs. 'What is it this time?'

'I doubt if a clever girl like you really has to ask,' he answered with a grin. 'Shall we say, I've come to my senses?'

'Harry!' Fenella appeared at the kitchen door. She was wearing an apron too and was clutching a cookery book to her breast. She looked rosy and vivid and flustered. 'Harry, this thing's going to boil over in another moment.'

'Oh, my darling, how perfectly lovely and useless you are!' he cried happily. 'All right, you can let it boil over and make a mess of the stove, or you can take it off the stove before it does—take your choice.'

'Oh, Harry, please!' she said anxiously.

He made a rapier-like pass at her with the kitchen knife, just missing her face, then darted into the kitchen. Fenella gave Caroline a self-conscious smile and followed him.

A moment later he put his head out of the kitchen door again.

'Caroline, have I ever told you my theory that if you can read, you can cook?' he said.

110

'It's how I learnt myself. I just read cookery books. But it doesn't work with Fenella. Yet she's clever at some things with those preposterous hands of hers. I've seen her take the vacuum cleaner apart and put it together again. I think she's probably an inhibited artist of some sort.'

There was another wail from inside the kitchen and he vanished again.

Laughing as she went up to her room, Caroline thought that there had really been no need to ask what they were celebrating.

She would have felt more like celebrating herself if she had not had that glimpse of the green van and its driver at the bottom of the hill.

Taking off her coat, she kicked off her shoes and lay down on the bed. If she had a good rest, she thought, and if the meal which Harry and Fenella, in their state of exalted emotion, were busy concocting together turned out as appetising as it smelled, she might feel up to going out with them. Meanwhile, she knew that she had to decide, and fairly quickly, what she meant to do about Jack Dawson. For if she did not tell the police almost at once that she had seen him, it would soon become very difficult to tell them so at all. She would find herself almost forced into supporting Jan Pullen's lies about him.

Reaching for a cigarette, she lit it and lay back again.

Suppose, she thought, she told the police that she had seen the van at the garage. Suppose she told them the story that Jan had told her. Would he admit it when they questioned him again, or was he capable of denying it all? But even if he did deny it, wouldn't the police believe her? If they had to choose between her story and Jan's, wouldn't they take for granted that she was the more reliable witness? Well, perhaps, but wasn't that what most people thought about themselves?

She gave a wry smile up at the ceiling, watching the faint trail of smoke from her cigarette drifting across it.

Jan could always remind them that she had just been in an unpleasant accident. Probably, he could say to them, her nerves were still in such a state that she was liable to see the face of the van-driver everywhere. Yes, but why should he say anything of the kind? Why was she so dubious about him? She could easily imagine herself, if she had suddenly been attacked by Harry with wild accusations, trying to make him stop it by saying the first thing that came into her head, true or not. And then possibly she would have felt that she had better say the same thing to the police. If that was all that Jan had done, she wasn't inclined to blame him. So what did she really feel was wrong with him?

His hammering in the night? The locked shed behind the garage, with the sacking stretched across the window? His painful love for Fenella? The mystery of why a man like him had turned his back on the world that he had grown up in and hidden himself here? Or simply the suspicion that Harry had done his best to cast on him? Had Harry been successful, in his jealousy, in sowing a little poison in her mind?

She did not like the thought of that and shifted back from worrying about Jan Pullen's character to wondering what she ought to do about Jack Dawson. She really ought to go and see him, as Jan had suggested. Only not now. Not today. She was far too tired. As Jan perhaps had realised that she would be, though the thought of doing it might delay her going to the police . . .

Dinner was early that evening. Fenella came up presently to warn Caroline and to find out if she felt up to going out with them.

'It isn't going to be much of a celebration,' she said. 'We're only going to a cinema. And Mr. Sherwin's taking us in his car. He and Mrs. Dewhurst are arguing about what we ought to go and see. He says he's incapable of sitting through anything but a Western, with lots of riding and shooting and smashing up saloons, and Mrs. Dewhurst says she'd like to see a nice film, about nice people, who have some nice children, or perhaps a nice dog.'

'And which will it be?' Caroline asked.

'Neither. You'll see.'

What Fenella meant by that, Caroline soon realised when she went downstairs, was that the choice of what they were to see would be made by Harry, a Harry so gay, so triumphantly in love with his slightly embarrassed but apparently happy wife that no one could possibly have denied him anything he wanted.

He studied an evening paper that Mr. Sherwin had brought back with him, then told them that there was a murder film at the Grand, which he had read about some time ago and had meant to make a point of seeing when it came to Rudbourne.

'I'm sure it's the only thing worth seeing,' he said, going on, as a matter of form, to ask them if they didn't agree.

No one dreamt of arguing.

It was only a few minutes afterwards, however, that Mrs. Dewhurst first complained of a headache. Her plump face began to look paler than usual under the pink and white make-up.

'I'm so sorry, my dears,' she said, 'but I'm afraid it's going to be one of my bad ones. I slept so badly last night, that's the trouble. First there was all the worry, and then the excitement, and then there was that dreadful hammering. Can't anything be done about that? Please!'

Mr. Sherwin gave a slight start. 'I was going to speak to Pullen about it, wasn't I? I'm sorry, it completely slipped my memory. But I'll do it tomorrow.'

'If it goes on, I can't stay, I simply can't!' she moaned, leaning her head on her hands and shutting her eyes. 'And tonight you must go without me. It's too bad, I was so looking forward to it, but I just can't help it.'

Harry and Fenella exchanged glances.

'Is it the idea of a film about murder that you don't like, Mrs. Dewhurst?' Harry asked. His voice was mild and flat, but there was a curious gleam in his eyes.

'Oh, dear me, no,' she answered, almost sobbing by now. 'Please don't worry about me. Just go out and enjoy yourselves. I'll take some aspirins and go to bed, and hope and pray that young man doesn't start hammering.'

She stood up shakily and left the room.

Fenella gave an irritated sigh. 'It always happens, doesn't it? What hell she must have been to live with. For her husband, I mean. Think how he must have felt if she got one of those headaches every time he suggested going out.'

'Perhaps she didn't get them in those days,' Harry said. 'She may not have needed them.'

'Ah, let's not start that tonight!' Fenella said quickly. 'Poor Mrs. Dewhurst, I absolutely refuse to believe there's any reason why she should be afraid of being seen in Rudbourne. Actually I'm awfully sorry for her. The headaches are perfectly genuine. I've seen her swallowing handfuls of aspirins for them.'

'I only meant,' Harry said, still in the same expressionless voice and with the same intent look in his eyes, 'that they're neurotic, which means she gets them when she wants them. Just why she wants them is anybody's guess. It could be anything from frustrated sex to remorse for having poisoned poor Mr. Dewhurst.'

'You're horrid,' Fenella said, 'she hasn't poisoned anybody. Anyway, there's no point in worrying about her. This started as a celebration. Let's enjoy it.'

And in a quiet way, they did enjoy it. Harry's choice of a film had been a good one. It was full of mysterious tension between the characters and there were one or two moments of explosive terror. Harry held Fenella's hand all the evening, nuzzling it gently from time to time, and afterwards they sat in the back of the car together, while Caroline sat in front with Mr. Sherwin. Harry kept his arm round Fenella, whispering in her ear and laughing softly at what she answered.

Glancing at Caroline, Mr. Sherwin smiled and murmured, ' "On such a night . . ." '

Caroline smiled back. It had been his swift action in the morning, she remembered, when he had invited her to go to Rudbourne with him, that had given Harry and Fenella the chance to have their quarrel out in private and arrive at this obviously satisfactory conclusion.

All the same, Caroline thought, what a mistake they had made when Harry gave up his job and they started the guesthouse. For it meant that they had almost no private life. There would always be an audience to observe everything that went on between them, and neither of them was so self-controlled, so stable, that there wouldn't always be clashes, or that there was any hope of their being able to hide the clashes when they happened. And sometimes the audience wouldn't be as perceptive as Hugh Sherwin, as self-effacing as Emma Dewhurst. The venture seemed to have been doomed, once you considered it from that angle, from the very start. For a year or two Harry and Fenella might struggle on, making believe that they loved their old house too much to leave it, but sooner or later something would blow up. They would sell the place and Harry would go back to journalism.

It did not occur to Caroline that for reasons quite different from these of which she was thinking, the doom of the guesthouse was already upon it. As she looked out of the car at the long, smooth scallops that the downs cut out of the starry sky, at the hedges that were suddenly richly green in the brilliance of the headlights, then lost in darkness, that everything was already over. Even when they stopped at the garage, where Mr. Sherwin was going to get out to ask Jan Pullen to desist from his hammering that night, she did not

117

notice the strange redness in the sky beyond the cutting.

It was Hugh Sherwin who saw it first and yelled, 'That's fire!'

Instead of getting out, he sent the car shooting forward to the top of the hill, crested it with a sickening bump, tore on downhill and lurched in through the stone gateposts, missing one of them by inches.

Above the noise of the racing motor, Fenella shrieked, 'Where's Mrs. Dewhurst?'

The car stopped and the bookseller leapt out. But even before it had stopped, Harry was out of it, racing towards the house. There was a roaring sound in the air and sparks danced dizzily high in the night sky. The stench of burning was horrible.

Harry reached the front door and threw it open.

Fenella called something wildly after him, but he did not look back. With an arm up before his face, he vanished into the red light inside.

CHAPTER NINE

The fire was all at one end of the long, low house, the end where Mrs. Dewhurst's bedroom was. Smoke was pouring out from her window and the roof above it was in

118

flames.

Fenella ran after Harry. She was still shrieking something, but the words were lost in the roaring sound that filled the air.

She was almost at the door when Hugh Sherwin caught up with her. She struggled with him when he tried to hold her back, wrenched herself free and vanished into the house. He went in after her.

Much slower than the others, Caroline was starting to follow them when she had the idea that the most useful thing that she could do was to drive to the nearest telephone to summon help. The nearest telephone that she knew of was at Jan Pullen's garage. She turned back to the car and was just getting into it again when she realised that a high, clanging sound coming out of the night was the bell of a fire-engine. Someone had already seen the fire and had given the alarm.

Probably, she thought, it had been Mrs. Dewhurst. It was to be hoped so, for if she had not got out in time, had not got downstairs to the telephone, where was she? With a chill in her veins, in spite of the puffs of heat that came to her from the burning house, Caroline started towards it.

At that moment she heard running footsteps in the drive behind her. Jan Pullen passed close to her, making for the house. Just as he reached it, Fenella came out. From where Caroline was it looked as if Fenella walked straight into his arms and clung to him. Then she tore herself away and would have gone back into the house if Hugh Sherwin, who had come out just after her, had not caught her and thrust her back at Jan. At the same time he saw Caroline and shouted something at her. Then he went running towards the garage. She had not heard what he said, but decided to follow him.

By the time that she reached the garage, he had the doors open and was lifting down the extending ladder that hung on some iron hooks on the wall. When she went to help him, he told her sharply to leave it to him, but she grasped one end of the ladder and stumbled along after him, though she found it much heavier than it looked. When Jan Pullen saw them coming and took Caroline's end of it from her, she was gasping and dizzy with weakness. Something that the bright young doctor in the hospital had said to her was ringing in her head. 'A little quiet housework won't hurt you, but don't try moving the grand piano.' For some reason this now struck her as incredibly funny. She wanted to tell Mr. Sherwin about it and make him laugh. But she had no breath to spare for speaking.

'The bathroom window,' Fenella shouted, as the two men started to raise the ladder against the wall of the house. 'Look—that's where they are!'

It was at least where Harry was. They all

saw him there, leaning out and cheerily waving. Then abruptly he disappeared.

Fenella gave a cry. She turned to Caroline and hid her face against her.

Caroline tried to tell her that there was nothing to worry about, that Harry was in no danger. For there was no red glare at that window, no smoke pouring out. The fire had not yet spread from the other end of the house.

'But Mrs. Dewhurst—what's happened to her?' Fenella wailed.

'She must be all right,' Caroline said. 'Harry wouldn't have waved like that if anything awful had happened.'

'Where is she then?'

'Probably not in there at all. I should think she just gave the alarm and bolted.'

'Jan gave the alarm. He just told me. He said he saw the fire in the sky and came straight here. But he thought we'd all gone out, and the telephone wouldn't work, so he went back to the garage to call the fire-brigade . . . Oh, Harry, Harry, Harry!' Fenella was looking at the house again, but still holding on tight to Caroline and shaking all over. Suddenly her voice shot up in a scream of terror and hope. 'There they are!'

Harry was at the bathroom window again, with Emma Dewhurst in his arms, and Mr. Sherwin was climbing up the ladder towards them. At the same time the fire-engines turned in at the gate and men in helmets came racing towards the house.

As the hiss of water cut sharply through the crackle of the flames, one of the firemen climbed up the ladder after Mr. Sherwin, who helped Harry to load Mrs. Dewhurst on to the man's shoulders. She was in a blue dressing-gown and had her black hair done up on rollers. From her utter limpness as the fireman brought her briskly down, it was plain that she was unconscious.

Caroline ran to the car and got a rug out of it. She spread it on the ground and the fireman laid Mrs. Dewhurst down on it. With a little moan, she opened her eyes and stared up at him blankly.

Fenella exclaimed, 'She's alive!'

'Of course she's alive!' Harry had followed the fireman down and was standing beside him, mopping his face. It was red and sweating and streaked with black. 'The damned fool, why couldn't she do something about the fire?'

Perhaps Mrs. Dewhurst heard him. She moaned again.

He turned his back on her and stared at the house. Instead of the cheerfulness that had shown on his face while he had still been in the burning building, there was bitter anger. He looked as if he were deciding who was to be made to suffer for what had happened. But for once he seemed to have used up all his vitality. His shoulders slumped and his breath came with difficulty. When Fenella held out her arms to him, he did not seem to notice. When she put them round him, he did not move, but only went on staring over her shoulder at the house.

'Are you all right, Harry?' she asked. 'Harry, Harry—are you hurt?'

On the rug Mrs. Dewhurst shifted her head a little and muttered, 'The man . . .'

One of her hands began to move up her body, exploring the buttons of her dressing-gown, making sure that she was decent.

Caroline knelt down beside her. 'Where are you hurt, Mrs. Dewhurst?'

'Emma,' she murmured faintly.

'Emma—where are you hurt?' Caroline repeated.

With a snarl in his voice, Harry said, 'She isn't hurt at all. She just lost her head and fainted, instead of doing something sensible about the fire.'

'Not much she could have done, if she didn't wake up in time,' Mr. Sherwin said, and walked off towards a group of the firemen, shadowy figures seen through swirling smoke. He was breathing unevenly after his unusual exertions, but managed to look as neat and precise as ever.

'Where did you find her, Harry?' Jan Pullen asked.

'At the top of the stairs, all in a damned heap,' Harry said. 'And when I spoke to her, she said, "Call me Emma!" God Almighty!'

At that moment one of the firemen called to Harry, asking him to come and look at something that they had found.

He did not stir, so Fenella went instead of him, and Jan, when he found that Harry had nothing to say to him, went after her.

Emma Dewhurst's lips moved again, weakly wriggling it the midst of her pale face.

'There was a man . . . I heard him . . . I went to see . . .' she whimpered. 'Oh, my head, my head!'

Harry turned at once, as if this were what he had been waiting for, and knelt down beside her.

'A man, Emma? What sort of man?'

Caroline frowned at him. 'We ought to get a doctor,' she whispered.

He took no notice. 'What was he like, Emma? Tell me, it's important.'

She moaned again. 'I didn't see him properly. He hit me. Oh, my poor head!'

'Come on, come on!' Harry's lassitude had gone. His slightly bulging, brilliant eyes were shining with excitement. 'Was he a big man, a small man, old, young, dark, fair?'

She turned her head away from him on the rug and did not answer.

'We've got to get a doctor for her,' Caroline said. 'That one who came to see me yesterday—what's his number? I'll go to the garage and ring up.'

124

With surprising speed, one of Mrs. Dewhurst's plump hands shot out and gripped her arm.

'Don't go!' she cried. 'Please, dear, don't leave me!'

Harry gave a harsh laugh. 'I told you she wasn't hurt. It's just some more of her bloody hysteria.'

'Well,' Caroline said, 'she's terribly scared.'

'And why shouldn't she be scared,' he demanded brutally, 'when for all we know she set the house on fire herself? Our house, our beautiful house, remember?'

He turned on his heel and walked off after Jan and Fenella.

Emma Dewhurst gave a long sigh. She sat up, bending forward and taking her head in her hands.

'Oh, I hope he won't come back,' she said with a shudder. 'You won't leave me, will you, dear? I'm so horribly frightened.'

'You're frightened of Harry?' Caroline said incredulously. 'But he pulled you out of the fire.'

'Did he? . . . Who? . . .' Mrs. Dewhurst's eyes fastened blearily on Caroline's face, as if at last they were trying to see her clearly. 'Oh, you mean Harry! Did he really? I'm so confused. I meant frightened of the man I heard in the house. But sometimes Harry frightens me too. The things he says . . .'

'Never mind that,' Caroline said. 'Just wait a

minute—I'll see if there's another rug in the car. You ought to have something over you.'

'No—please!' Fear leapt into Mrs. Dewhurst's eyes again, making them blank and stupid. 'You—you did say Mr. Lyddon pulled me out of the fire, didn't you?'

Caroline told her what Harry had done.

'Well!' Mrs. Dewhurst said with another long sigh and sank back again on the rug. 'That's different. He's wonderfully brave, isn't he? And I didn't thank him. I didn't say a word. No wonder he got angry with me.'

'He didn't really get angry with you,' Caroline said, 'just with his bad luck. He loved this house.'

She was thinking that until that night she had not done justice to Harry's love for the house, the home that was to help him put down roots.

'He's wonderfully brave,' Mrs. Dewhurst repeated. 'But I must tell him I didn't start the fire. Just think of it—*me*! Poor boy, what an idea to have in his head. I hope I can make him believe me.'

'He believes you already.' But the words came out with less conviction than Caroline would have liked. Harry, she thought, was only too likely to decide that someone had done this thing on purpose to spite him. 'Now you aren't still feeling frightened, are you? Because you've simply got to let me find you a coat or something.'

126

Fenella came up just then with a coat over her arm. It was a blue coat with a small collar of Persian lamb.

'Here you are,' she said. 'It's yours, isn't it, Mrs. Dewhurst?'

'Yes, dear. How thoughtful of you. Thank you so much,' Mrs. Dewhurst answered, as Fenella draped it round her shoulders. Then the cloudy look came back to her eyes. 'But— where did you find it? Wasn't it . . .? All my things, aren't they burnt?'

'Don't you remember?' Fenella said. 'You managed to throw most of them out of the window. There's a heap of them there. That's what the firemen wanted us to come and look at.'

'I—threw them out—of the window?' Mrs. Dewhurst said incredulously.

'And nearly got burnt yourself instead, which wasn't very clever, was it?' Fenella said.

'No,' Mrs. Dewhurst said, and began to cry. 'And so your dear Harry risked his life for me. Oh, what must he think of me. I must have been quite out of my mind. I can't remember any of it.'

Whatever Harry thought of her, he at least did not accuse her again of having started the fire, or even of being seriously to blame for having failed to put it out. He seemed so relieved, after the first shock, to find that the damage done to the house was less than he had thought to begin with, that he was able to

127

convince himself that he was in luck after all, and his heart began to overflow with thankfulness and loving kindness.

In fact, the only serious damage proved to be in the rooms at the end of the house and to the roof above them. The rooms were Mrs. Dewhurst's bedroom and a small room always referred to as Harry's study, although he hardly ever used it, and the long sitting-room under them. All these, the firemen said, were unsafe. But the staircase had been saved before it had done more than start to smoulder on the top few steps and the main part of the house was unharmed. Everything in the remaining rooms was covered with a black film of soot and they were pervaded with a sickening smell of burnt varnish and charred wood, but as Harry and Fenella and their three guests sat drinking tea in the kitchen, they were all ready to ignore the discomforts and start counting their mercies.

They went on counting them, with the unnecessary repetitiveness that afflicts people who are recovering from shock, until Harry said, 'But now we want to hear all about the man Emma says she saw. Come on, Emma, tell us all about him.'

It was nearly two in the morning. The firemen had gone and so had the doctor, who had treated Harry for a few burns and Mrs. Dewhurst for a bruise on the head. Jan Pullen had gone and so had the villagers who had poured up the road to help and to enjoy the excitement. A number of them had made offers of beds for the night, but Harry and Fenella had been determined to stay in their house, which had settled the matter for Caroline, and apparently also for Emma Dewhurst and Hugh Sherwin.

'I did see him, I really did,' Mrs. Dewhurst replied to Harry. 'I mean, I *heard* him.'

'When?' he asked.

'I don't know,' she said. 'I'd been asleep for some time. Suddenly I woke up with a start, knowing I'd heard a noise. You know how one does. I didn't know what the noise was. Then I heard it again. Footsteps. Very soft, careful footsteps.'

'So you got up to investigate? Brave Emma!' Harry grinned. 'Did you know that when I found you at the top of the stairs, you asked me to call you Emma?'

'Oh, Mr. Lyddon, you're making that up,' she said.

'No, *I'm* not making anything up,' he said, still with a good-humoured but mocking little smile. 'And after all we've been through together, I think you might call me Harry— and explain why you didn't just decide you were hearing us come home.'

He was casting doubt on her story, Caroline thought, simply to get it out of her. Behind his amusement he was very intent, very impatient to hear the rest of it.

'Oh, you're never as quiet as that,' Mrs. Dewhurst said. 'Besides, when I peeped out of my door, there weren't any lights on anywhere.'

'So the fire hadn't started yet.'

'No, of course not. I don't know when the fire started. It was after—after—' Her face went blank and she started to twist her fingers together.

Harry patted her shoulder. 'Don't worry, Emma, the man isn't here now. Nobody's going to hurt you.'

She smiled up at him. The sudden radiance on her face made her look quite girlish.

'Oh, Harry, I still haven't thanked you properly for what you did,' she said. 'It was so wonderfully brave of you. When I think—when I try to think—of what would have happened to me—'

'Don't try,' Harry said quickly. 'It's wonderfully brave Emma we're concentrating on at the moment. You were just peeping out of the door and everything was dark. What happened next?'

'I crept along the passage to the top of the stairs,' she said.

'The footsteps were downstairs, then?'

'Yes.'

'Did you go down?'

'Oh no.'

'Then whoever it was came up to meet you.'

'Ye-es,' she said uncertainly. 'I suppose he

must have.'

'Can't you remember? You were upstairs when I found you. You were in the passage between your bedroom and my study.'

'Yes, I—I tried to run away. I remember that. I heard him coming and I saw . . .' She looked puzzled. 'No, I didn't really see him. It was too dark.'

'Couldn't you even tell if he was big or small?'

'I think—I think he was big. But I'm not sure. I'm not sure of anything after that, except that I owe my life to you, Harry.' Suddenly she clasped one of his hands in both of hers. If he had not snatched it sharply away, she would have pressed it to her lips. 'I think you're the best man I ever met, the bravest and kindest.'

Looking distinctly frightened of her, Harry edged swiftly out of reach.

'That's fine, Emma,' he said. 'I absolutely agree with you. I only wish more other people did.'

It was said laughingly, but his eyes were sombre. Muttering that they all wanted more tea, he picked up the kettle and took it to the sink to refill it.

Almost for the first time since he had come into the kitchen and said thank you for the first cup of tea that Harry had given him, Hugh Sherwin spoke. 'How did the fire start, Lyddon? A fault in the wiring?'

CHAPTER TEN

Harry was, or made a show of being, too preoccupied to hear the question. He had the look of someone with a problem on his mind that had to be solved before he could think about anything else.

'Anyway, it could have been far worse,' Fenella said. She was watching him with something in her expression that Caroline had never seen there before, a glow that made her think of how Fenella must have felt when she had seen Harry rescue the child from the river, however angry she had afterwards pretended to be about her crumpled radiator. 'There was nothing of any real value in any of those rooms.'

'Nothing of ours,' Harry said. 'Only some cheap furniture and some files and a few reference books. But I don't know what Emma's lost.'

Emma Dewhurst shook her head. 'Nothing that matters, dear—nothing compared with what I've got to be thankful for.'

'What about those files?' Mr. Sherwin asked. 'And there was a desk in the study, wasn't there? What about the papers inside them?'

'You're thinking of manuscripts?' Harry said with a short laugh. 'No, there were only a few that had been the rounds and been turned down by everyone.'

'Nothing else?' Mr. Sherwin persisted. 'Nothing important?'

'Important . . .?' Harry shrugged his shoulders. 'My birth certificate, my passport, some things like that. I suppose I can get duplicates.'

'I was thinking of the ones you told us about yesterday,' Mr. Sherwin said. 'Those records you said you'd made of all the dangerous things you know.'

'Oh, for God's sake!' Harry said, as if the bookseller ought to have known better than to take him seriously.

Caroline wondered what Mr. Sherwin made of it. She herself was a good deal puzzled. For, remembering the man whom Mrs. Dewhurst had heard on the stairs, it did not seem to her too improbable that he had lit the fire on purpose to destroy those records of Harry's.

Suddenly Caroline seemed to see the man, to see him with remarkable vividness, to know exactly what he looked like. He was big and paunchy, was slightly bald, had curious eyes, not quite on the same level, flashing false teeth and hands like hams. And the little finger on his left hand had been broken.

But it was quite as likely to have been the small man with the foxy face. Or neither of them.

Or had they both been there? While Mrs.

Dewhurst had been at the top of the stairs, listening to the footsteps in the darkness below her, had she been struck down from behind by someone who was already upstairs? Was that why she could not remember seeing him?

Caroline found this a very plausible theory, but she did not mention it to anyone else that night. They were all far too tired to think coherently. She helped Fenella to make up a bed for Mrs. Dewhurst in one of the empty bedrooms in the undamaged part of the house, then went to bed herself and fell at once into an exhausted, dreamless sleep. She slept until late in the morning, only waking when Harry, who had just come to her bedside with her breakfast on a tray, shouted her name at her.

Opening heavy eyes, Caroline grunted sleepily that she could easily have gone downstairs to breakfast.

'I know, I know,' Harry said with one of his vivid smiles. He was wearing his striped cooking apron over a pullover and flannels and looked as fresh and brisk as if he had had a normal amount of sleep and hadn't a care in the world. 'But we promised you you could convalesce here, so you're damned well going to do some convalescing, like it or not. And the house is full of police and insurance assessors and such like, whom I don't suppose it's your life's ambition to meet.'

Caroline sat up in the bed.

'Do they know yet how the fire started?' she

asked.

Harry put the tray down on her knees.

'They seem to think it must have been a short in the flex of the reading-lamp on my desk,' he said. 'Anything else you want? Sugar, butter, marmalade—I think it's all there.'

'Yes, of course. But wait a minute, Harry—'

'If you're going to say, "Serves me right",' he interrupted, 'after the things I've said about Sherwin's fire, go ahead and say it. I'll grovel as much as you like. Of course it serves me right.'

Caroline poured out a cup of coffee. 'I was going to say, what about the man Mrs. Dewhurst saw? How does he fit in if it really began with a short?'

'How indeed?' He grinned again, but this time there was something the matter with the grin. His mouth performed, but his eyes were guarded. 'I suppose a knock on the head does queer things to you. Anyway, it was luck for us Jan saw the fire. If the fire brigade hadn't got here so fast we'd have lost the whole place.'

He turned to the door.

'No, wait,' Caroline said again. 'You think it's queer, don't you, that Mrs. Dewhurst can't remember the man coming upstairs? But I think I've got an explanation for that, Harry.'

'Caroline, there simply wasn't any man, that's all I mean,' he said.

'But suppose there were two men,' she insisted. 'Doesn't that make sense? Because

135

one of them could have been upstairs already when she came out of her room and could have knocked her out while she was listening to the other one walking about below.'

Harry shook his head. 'There wasn't any man. The knock on the head, or shock, or something, set Emma's imagination going.'

'I'd never have suspected she had any,' Caroline said.

'You live and learn.'

'But how did she get the knock on the head?'

'Hitting the edge of the old chest in the passage when the smoke overcame her.'

She gave him a frowning look. 'Do you *know* that, Harry, or are you just guessing?'

'It stands to reason,' he answered a little evasively. 'Look, I'll tell you what happened. It's all quite simple. There was a short in the flex and it started sparking. The wood of the desk caught and started smouldering. The assessor fellow I've been talking to says it might have taken quite a time to get going. Then at some point something wakened Emma. It may have been the noise of the fire or the smell of burning. She went to see what was happening, then dashed back into her room and started throwing her belongings out of the window. But she'd left things a little late for getting away. When she realised that and made a dash for it, the passage was full of smoke and she collapsed. That can't have been

136

more than a minute or two before we got back. Anyway, you can take my word for it, there wasn't any man.'

'I'm afraid I still don't see why you're so sure there wasn't,' Caroline said. 'There've been two mysterious men hanging around, haven't there?'

Harry's hand dropped from the door-handle. He stared at her for a moment with a curious blankness, then came back to her bedside.

'And there's something else,' she said. 'When we came back here, after the accident, and I'd got into bed and Fenella had just gone downstairs to meet the doctor, Mrs. Dewhurst came in to see me and she asked me a very strange thing. She asked me if I'd been wearing my blue coat when the accident happened.'

'Well?' Harry said.

She thought that she had never met anyone who could make his face quite as expressionless as Harry could when he chose.

'Well, she's got a blue coat herself,' she said. 'Just like you, she was afraid the van had smashed into us on purpose, only she thought it was because they were after her.'

'Let's go back to the two men,' Harry said. 'One was upstairs and one was down—is that it? And while she was listening to the one walking about downstairs, the other one bopped her on the head. Then they set fire to the place, but kindly took the trouble to throw her belongings out of the window for her.'

'Perhaps they were after something they thought she'd got.'

He gave her another long, blank look and then an embarrassed smile.

'D'you know, Caroline, you're making me feel pretty bad. I'm sorry. I know I oughtn't to talk the sort of rot I do. It's just something that gets into me now and then, I don't even know why. People who really know me never take any notice of it.'

'But suppose those two men came here to burn up these records—'

'Oh God!' He clutched his head. 'How am I ever going to get this straightened out? I'm a fool, I'm crazy, I'm probably certifiable—can't you grasp that? Why should anyone bother to burn my records? I could write all the stuff down again this minute out of my head.'

'But some records did really exist, didn't they, Harry?' she said. 'They weren't just talk too?'

'Well, of course I've got a lot of old notes and cuttings, but I'm afraid they aren't quite the dynamite I tried to make out the other evening. I was distinctly above myself just then. Everyone telling me how clever I'd been, saving our lives, must have gone to my head.'

'Yet saving Emma Dewhurst's life seems to have had the opposite effect.'

'Hmm,' Harry said, frowning at her, 'that, in

its way, is an uncomfortably penetrating remark. So I think I'll tell you something. Try to tell you.' He looked round, reached for a chair and drew it up to Caroline's bedside. 'You can believe it or not, as you choose. I really wasn't thinking about Emma or my blasted records when I dashed into the house. I was thinking about the house itself and nothing else. I was thinking there might be something I could do to save it. If there had been, I'm not sure I shouldn't have left Emma where she was.'

'Only there wasn't, and you didn't, and I don't think I do believe you about that,' Caroline said.

'Yet you don't know me very well, do you? You don't know much about what makes me tick.'

She felt inclined to say that she doubted if he did himself, but only gave a slight shake of her head.

'No,' he said, as if an important point had been proved, 'and I don't think Fenella does either. She may even know less about it than you do, because she started out with certain preconceived notions. You can't think what a bother they've been to me—except that you've lived with her misconceptions about you, so perhaps you know what I mean.'

'About me? Such as?'

'Well, why do you think we kept out of your way so pointedly for so long?'

'I suppose you found you could get on without me.'

'And only got in touch with you when there was something Fenella—or perhaps both of us—wanted from you? Well, that remark's nearer to the sort of thing Fenella told me you said all the time than anything I've heard you say yet. After all I'd heard from her, you didn't seem to me at all a fearsome sort of person. You seemed quite tolerant and quite uninterfering, in fact, quite nice to have around, dear Caroline, if you see what I mean.'

'I'm not sure that I do, and I think we're straying from the point,' she said.

'No, we aren't. The point at the moment is that if Fenella can be as wrong about you as she seems to be telling me, I mean, that you'd dislike me sight unseen, simply because she'd fallen in love with me, that you'd despise me for having given up my job, that you'd try to come between us by criticising us to each other and telling me a lot of things about her which we've decided there's no need for me to know—'

'Did she really say those things about me?' Caroline interrupted.

'Oh yes, and lots more, when she wasn't telling me what a model of the virtues you were. It just depended on the mood she was in. But you can judge the sort of muddle her poor mind is in about you, because you know how wrong that all is. Well, she's in an even worse

140

muddle about me. She sees me, or she used to see me, as a lunatic kind of hero, who in between saving lots of lives in nicely conspicuous circumstances and generally impressing people—even, at last, her terribly superior sister—was going to toss off some literary gem every little while . . . Why are you staring at me like that, Caroline?'

She dropped her eyes to the tray on her knees and poured out another cup of coffee with a hand that was not quite steady. The truth was that for a moment or two she had almost ceased to see him, while she pondered the problem of why it should hurt so much to be told something which, after all, she had known for many years. She had never had any illusions about what Fenella thought of her. Fenella herself had told her, with varying degrees of violence, all too many times, and Caroline had come to be able to think of it as probably partly justified, and, for the rest, unimportant. But still, it was astonishing how it hurt to think of her pouring out all the old complaints to Harry.

Hoping that this did not show in either her face or her voice, she said, 'So you're really sure there weren't any men in the house last night.'

'Don't try changing the subject,' he said. 'I'm trying to tell you something rather important.'

'It's you who've changed the subject,' she

said.

'No. It was just a bit of a digression. I'm getting round to explaining to you why I'm not more elated at having saved that damned woman's life—if I did. I mean, if I hadn't, someone else would have made just as good a job of it. Sherwin, perhaps, or Jan. And either of them might have had some reason to be proud of himself. But I haven't, because I didn't come in to save her, I came in to save the house. You see, whatever Fenella may have told you about our having come here so that I could write is all upside down. I'm going to write so that we can go on living here. Living here, living in this house, is what matters to me. You don't know how much it matters!'

He stood up and started walking up and down the room. There was a slight flush on his face, as if he were even more stirred than he wanted to admit.

'My father was an army doctor,' he said. 'D'you know what that means? It meant eternal moving from place to place, Egypt, India, Burma. Then a boarding school in England and holidays with an aunt in Leeds. Only glimpses of my parents now and then. But always talk of the time when my father would get out of the army and settle down in a nice old house like the one he grew up in and we'd have a real home at last. Then his dying and my mother coming to live with her sister in Leeds and the two of them somehow getting swindled out of the little money they had, so that I had to get a job as fast as I could and stick to it, never taking any risks, never striking out for myself, till they'd both died too. Do I sound brutal? I don't mind much if I do. They were all such well-meaning people, so kind, so good, and they gave me the kind of childhood I'm not going to inflict on any child of mine if I have to stick to cooking for the rest of my life—if I have to take to crime!' He caught his breath sharply, then switched on his brilliant smile. 'I needn't really have poured all that out, need I? But d'you understand now why I'm so angry with that fool of a woman? Think of her actually rushing to throw her stuff out of the window, instead of ringing up the fire brigade, or even throwing a few buckets of water on the fire!'

'But if she'd been knocked unconscious . . .'

He laughed harshly. 'For God's sake, can you imagine Emma getting up to investigate strange noises downstairs? She'd be more likely to pull the bedclothes up over her head and start praying. No, the fire was caused by that damned reading-lamp. It was years old and the insulation on the flex was worn through. And I knew that. And that, you see, makes the whole thing my fault. So perhaps you see now why I'm not bounding around, handing out medals to myself.'

He snatched up her breakfast tray, strode to the door and went out.

143

He left Caroline very puzzled.

She did not know why it was, but the more that Harry refused to believe in the man whom Emma Dewhurst had heard in the darkness, the more she found herself believing in him. She was being like Fenella, who only took Harry seriously when he said he was joking. And in spite of Harry's explanations, Caroline felt that it was quite unlike him to be so determined to play down the drama of the fire. So what was his real reason for doing so?

Yet it was true that if the man, or men, had been after Harry's records, as Caroline had first guessed, it was difficult to explain why they should have thrown Mrs. Dewhurst's belongings out of the window. And if they had been after something of Mrs. Dewhurst's, why, once she was safely unconscious, had they set the house on fire? Simply to spite Harry? Or to cover up traces that they had left? Or had they thrown the things out of the window just on purpose to make people think what Harry was thinking, instead of seeing plainly that what had been meant to happen that night ...?

Suddenly Caroline threw the bedclothes back and sat up.

She did not want to stay alone there any longer, with no one to tell her what was wrong with her reasoning. She had to talk to someone immediately, someone who would reassure her that the last few days had obviously been too much for her and that quiet little widows like Emma Dewhurst didn't get murdered.

CHAPTER ELEVEN

Caroline dressed quickly, opened her door and went out into the passage. Dank and smoke-laden, a blast of cold air met her from the ruined end of the house. She shivered and went back to her room for her coat.

As she came out again, she realised that the whole house was full of voices. She could hear Sergeant Rutter talking to Mrs. Dewhurst, and some strange voices talking of building costs and insurance, and Fenella talking to Mrs. Freely about where they should start trying to clean up the mess, and Harry talking on the telephone to Jan Pullen, talking calmly and without any animosity about buying a new car. Only Hugh Sherwin was not talking to anybody. He had avoided it by going out into the garden. Caroline saw him from a window, walking up and down among the sad wreckage of the daffodils that had been trampled underfoot by firemen and helpers the night before.

He turned quickly when he heard her open the front door. He had a smear of soot on one cheek, of which he was plainly unaware, but in all other respects was as neat as usual. In one

145

hand he was twirling a red anemone that he had picked somewhere in the garden. When he met Caroline he handed it to her in an absent-minded way, as if handing red anemones to people were something that he frequently and casually did. In all probability, she thought, he did not even know that he had done it. He looked absorbed in his own thoughts and was swifter in starting to talk about them than Caroline was about hers.

'I'm glad you came out, Miss Dyer, because there's something I want to discuss with you,' he said, 'and I can't stand the house this morning. It isn't only the smell and the dirt that's intolerable, it's my exact knowledge of what comes next—each repulsive stage. The damp and the draughts, the mildew, the desolation. And they'll last for weeks. If I didn't feel it was the wrong time for me to clear out altogether, I think I'd move into a room at the Bull in Rudbourne.'

'Why is it the wrong time to leave?' Caroline asked. Not knowing what else to do with the anemone, she had put it into a buttonhole of her coat. 'I don't suppose Harry and Fenella would mind. It might even make things easier for them if we all left.'

'I wasn't actually thinking about the Lyddons,' he said. 'I was thinking strictly of myself. It seems to me it might be a bad time for me to leave when something's just got started here that hasn't finished.'

'I don't understand,' she said.

'Nor do I, nor do I,' he said. 'I just know there's something awfully wrong about this fire. Think of it—a fire, another fire, caused by defective wiring, and *I'm* here. How's that going to strike people?'

'You're much too sensitive about that,' she said. 'I don't see why they should be struck by it at all.'

'Even when Lyddon puts it into their minds?'

'But I don't think he will. He's quite made up his mind that the fire was started by a short in the flex of his reading-lamp, and that it's his own fault, if anyone's.'

He gave a curious smile. 'I think I'll feel safest if I'm on the spot to see he doesn't change his story. But that brings me to what I wanted to talk to you about. I've been thinking you ought to go home, Miss Dyer. Yesterday I suggested a Greek island to you and you wouldn't listen, but you've been ill, you're supposed to be taking care of yourself, and I can assure you, from experience, the next few days are going to be extremely uncomfortable. So why don't you go back to London?'

It was unreasonable, but the only thing that Caroline could think of when he said that was that he wanted her out of the way. He wanted to get rid of her. Her first feeling was dismay, then a heady little fizzing of anger started in her over-excited brain. With the least encouragement, she could have started to make a scene. Her fingers itched to push her sleeves up. They tried to clench into fists. Carefully she relaxed them. If she did make a scene, he would not have the faintest idea what it was all about. Nor would she herself, if it came to that. Besides, there was something else that she wanted to discuss with him.

But first she looked round and though there was no risk that what they were saying might be heard in the house, she thought that the way that they were standing there probably looked odd and conspicuous and was likely to draw attention to them. And at any moment someone might interrupt them. 'I'll think about it later,' she said. 'Meanwhile, shall we go for a walk?'

He turned obligingly towards the gate. 'I'd like you to think about it now,' he said.

'I'm afraid I've got something else on my mind,' she answered. 'You know Mrs. Dewhurst's story about the man she heard in the house last night?'

'Ah,' he said, as if he knew what was coming now.

'Well, what do you think about it?'

'Harry's been talking to you, hasn't he?' he said. 'He's decided there wasn't any man.'

'But you think there was,' she said eagerly. 'You don't agree with him.'

He walked on for a little way before he replied. 'I think I do agree with him, you know.

What I'm not sure of is whether Harry himself believes what he's been saying. Is it what he thinks, or is it merely what he wants everyone else to think?'

'Is that because you feel it's unlike him to pass up such a chance for drama?'

'Yes, he's playing everything down as hard as he can. Yet perhaps that's simply how he behaves when reality gets dramatic enough even for him. All the same . . .'

He paused. They had passed through the stone gateposts and turned down the lane in the direction that led away from the village.

'All the same,' he went on, 'he gave me the feeling of a man who's scared. Very badly scared.'

'Yes,' Caroline agreed quickly, realising that this was what she had felt herself.

'Perhaps for the first time in his life,' Mr. Sherwin said. 'I think, you know, that Lyddon's one of those curious, half-developed people who literally hardly know what fear is. So now he doesn't know what to do about it beyond pretending to himself and everyone else that there's no reason to be afraid.'

'And you think that actually there isn't,' Caroline said.

'Well, it seems to me just possible that Lyddon's at last managed to frighten himself with one of his fantasies, or perhaps got frightened *of* them in general—I mean of what they'll do to him if he doesn't learn to control

149

them.'

'But suppose they aren't fantasies, Mr. Sherwin.' She stood still, looking up at him. 'Do you remember saying to me that it would be surprising, with his intelligence, if he didn't hit the nail on the head occasionally?'

'Is that a way of telling me you think I'm a fire-raiser?'

'No,' she said impatiently. 'You aren't the only person Harry's spread suspicions about.'

'Because if it is,' he said, 'it suggests to me that what you've been through has been a little too much for you, which is another reason why you ought to go back to London.'

She smiled ironically. 'You seem to think it's quite natural for other people to think you're a fire-raiser, but if I do, things have been too much for me.'

He looked surprised for a moment. 'Yes,' he said. 'Yes, that's quite right. In the normal course of events, I should always expect sanity and a balanced judgment from you, Miss Dyer.'

'But what I'm trying to remind you of,' she said, wondering why she should find this remark somewhat irritating, when from anyone in the office she would have accepted it as quite simply her due, 'Harry's been telling people that Jan Pullen deals in stolen cars. He's tried to make us think that Mrs. Dewhurst's in hiding here, probably because she murdered her husband. Well, suppose it's true about Mrs. Dewhurst. I don't mean about the husband necessarily, but that she is hiding from someone or something.'

Mr. Sherwin did not answer, but she saw with satisfaction that his smile had gone.

She went on, 'You see, something very odd happened after that accident with the van that I didn't tell anyone about at the time. It seemed such a silly, absurd thing, it didn't seem worth saying anything about it. I told Harry about it this morning, but that's all. I was lying down and Fenella had just gone downstairs to let the doctor in. Mrs. Dewhurst came into my room. She seemed very distressed and I thought at first it was in case I was badly hurt. But really she seemed to want to know just one thing—had I been wearing this blue coat when I was in the car with Harry? Well, she's got a blue coat herself, and her hair's about the same colour as mine—'

'No, no, excuse me,' he interrupted, 'the general impression is totally different.'

'It would be near enough,' she said, 'if you only had a description to go by. And then it was that evening, you remember, that Mrs. Dewhurst got fearfully upset when Harry was talking nonsense about having enemies—or what we thought was nonsense. She said how terrible it was to have an enemy. And last night, when she'd just recovered consciousness, she begged me not to leave her, because she was so afraid of the man she'd seen. And she really was afraid, that's one thing I'm quite sure of.'

'But you know about her throwing her things out of the window, don't you?' Mr. Sherwin said. 'So at least some of her story isn't true.'

'Unless she didn't throw them out. I mean, unless someone else did.'

He raised an eyebrow and smiled with mild derision. 'The man?'

'Why not?' she said defensively. 'Suppose those two men who've been round here, asking questions about everyone, were really looking for her. And suppose what they wanted was—was to get rid of Mrs. Dewhurst. Because that's what would have happened, she'd have been killed, if Harry hadn't rushed into the fire and saved her. And we'd all have thought, as you're thinking now, that she'd been overcome by the smoke and fallen and hit her head on the chest in the passage, after staying behind too long, trying to save her belongings . . . Oh, don't look so uninterested!'

'I'm not uninterested, not at all,' Mr. Sherwin answered gravely. 'I was just thinking . . . Please don't get angry with me, but I'm more convinced than ever that you ought to go back to London. By the next train, if possible.'

'Certainly not,' she said.

'Please, today.' He put an arm through hers and turned her back towards the house. 'Your sister will understand. In fact, as you said, she may be quite relieved to see you go. So if you'll pack up now, I'll drive you into Rudbourne.'

She resisted the pressure of his arm and stood rigidly where she was.

'Mr. Sherwin,' she said, 'I meant all those things I said.' It was at that moment that she became sure that she did mean them. 'I believe somebody tried to murder Mrs. Dewhurst last night.'

'I know you do, and I think you may even be right—that isn't the point,' he said.

'What is, then?'

'That, right or wrong, you've been very ill and you've got to have a chance to get better.'

'I'm allowed to do everything but move a grand piano!' she cried.

'Please!' he said. 'It *is* a grand piano, this burden you're trying to carry.'

He looked so anxious that just for a moment Caroline felt ready to do anything on earth he wanted. It took a great effort to say, 'No, I'm sorry, I'm not going anywhere.'

They eyed each other, each calculating the stubbornness, the potential awkwardness in the other.

Then Mr. Sherwin said, 'All right, what do we do next then? Take this idea of yours to the police?'

'There's something I'd like to do first,' she said. 'There's a man living somewhere in the village called Jack Dawson. I'd like to go and see him.'

'Shall I drive you there?'

'I'd be very grateful if you would.'

'But may I know why you want to see him?'

'He owns a green van, and I saw it again yesterday at Jan Pullen's garage, and he was talking to Jan. And Jan admitted to me he'd lied to Harry and the police about him, because the man was in too much trouble already. His wife left him suddenly and he started drinking and he's got some young children to look after—all of which may be true, but if it isn't, and if really he's connected with those other two men, then that accident was also an attempt to murder Mrs. Dewhurst, and the police ought to know all about it.'

'Of course you've seen that would mean that Pullen was involved in it too,' Mr. Sherwin said. 'Lyddon might even be right that it all has something to do with stolen cars. But before we go any further, perhaps I ought to repeat that really I still entirely agree with him about the fire. I think it was probably caused by a short in the flex of the reading-lamp. I don't think Mrs. Dewhurst heard any strange footsteps in the house. I don't think your accident with the van was anything but an accident. I don't think there's anything sinister about Pullen. The only thing that worries me seriously is the change in Lyddon. I'd like very much to know the real reason why he isn't thundering at us that the house was full of a whole gang of men last night, who'd come to burn up those records of his, and murder all of us into the bargain. Now if you'll wait while I get the car, we'll go and look for your man Dawson.'

He hurried on briskly ahead of her towards the house.

Following him as far as the gateway, Caroline stood there, waiting, exchanging stares with a cow that had come to gaze at her curiously over the hedge on the other side of the road.

Why, she was wondering, had she said nothing about her belief that Harry's records had not been burnt? She had told him of her other suspicions, so why had she said nothing about that one?

It was true that she had very little to go on. There was just the one remark that Harry had let drop. 'Of course I've got a lot of old notes and cuttings, but I'm afraid they aren't quite the dynamite I tried to make out the other evening . . .' That was all. And it could so easily have been a slip of the tongue, the sort of blunder that people often make about far more important matters. As, for instance, when they talk in the present tense of someone recently dead. All the same, Caroline felt a peculiar certainty that Harry had not made a mistake. She believed that his notes and cuttings had not gone up in flames, but were still wherever he had put them for safe keeping.

But what did that matter if she was right that the fire had been lit by the two unknown men, not for any reason connected with Harry's knowledge of them, but to conceal the attempted murder of Emma Dewhurst?

Mr. Sherwin's car came down the drive. He stopped it in the gateway.

'Where does this man Dawson live?' he asked, as Caroline got in beside him.

'I'm afraid all I know is that it's in what Jan Pullen called a rural slum,' she said, 'and I haven't seen anything that looks in the least like a slum in Dexter Abbas. But I suppose we can ask.'

'No, I don't think we'll need to, if that's what Pullen told you,' he said. 'There's a row of cottages at the end of the village which you've probably thought were charm itself, passing them by car. But in fact they've been condemned for years and ought to have been pulled down long ago. It's a scandal that nothing has been done yet about rehousing the unfortunate people living in them. That's probably the place.' He had turned out into the road and started up the hill towards the cutting. 'But I wonder just what you hope to accomplish by this visit, Miss Dyer. Suppose you find Dawson and his van and his children, just as Pullen told you, will you be any farther on than you were?'

'Only very little,' she admitted.

'Then why not listen to some advice, for a

156

change? Why not let me drive you back to the house for your luggage, then take you to the station?' He was driving very slowly, as if to give her a chance to tell him to stop. 'I wish you would.'

She laughed. She was beginning to enjoy his concern, to like the feeling of his worrying about her. It occurred to her that she had not had nearly enough of that sort of thing in her life.

'I can't,' she said. 'I simply can't.'

'Will you at least think about it?'

'Oh yes, I can do that.'

'I'm afraid you don't mean it,' he said resignedly. 'Well, tell me how Lyddon took it when you told him about having seen the van again.'

'I haven't told him.'

'For any special reason?'

'Mainly that there hasn't been much opportunity,' she said. 'When I got in after talking to Jan Pullen, I didn't want to say anything to spoil the mood Harry was in just then. Perhaps that was a bad mistake, but at the time it seemed the most important thing.'

'Yes,' he said, 'I'd probably have thought so too.'

'Then we all went out for the evening, and then there was the fire. And this morning Harry didn't want to be told about any mysterious green van.'

'I see.' He accelerated. Caroline saw that he

157

had given up the hope that she could be induced to change her mind about the visit to Jack Dawson.

As they drove between the high chalk walls of the cutting, left the garage behind and turned towards the village, he said nothing more. Passing the duck pond, the church and the post-office, they came to the last row of cottages. Such pretty cottages, white-walled and thatched. Mr. Sherwin had been right that Caroline had often admired them. Slowing down, he stopped the car a few feet short of a green van that stood in front of the last cottage in the row, a van that was in a very sorry state. Its bonnet had been smashed in. What was left of the windscreen was only a frame of jagged glass splinters. A tow-rope dangled from the bumper.

'It rather looks,' Mr. Sherwin observed, 'as if events have caught up with Jack Dawson.'

CHAPTER TWELVE

Caroline was thinking, 'So much for the chance Jan Pullen wanted me to give him!'

Getting out of the car, she stood for a moment looking at the row of cottages.

Seeing them from near at hand, she understood why Jan Pullen had called them a slum. The thatch that looked so charming if

158

you passed by fast enough was half-decayed and full of birds' nests. It was horrible to think of what happened under it in a heavy rain. Window frames and doors looked rotten. In some of the cottages a fierce struggle for respectability was being waged, with spotless curtains at the small windows, fresh paint on the crumbling woodwork and neat rows of wallflowers in the little front gardens. But in others squalor had conquered. Only the grime on the windows hid the bitterness inside. No money had been wasted on paint, or love lavished on the weed patches enclosed by the unmended fences.

Pushing open the gate of the last cottage in the row, Caroline went up to the door. She realised that not very long ago the garden must have been a source of great pride to someone. Besides the regulation wallflowers, there were forget-me-nots and round purple clumps of aubretia. There were rose bushes along the fence. Bronze buds of lilies were pushing up through the soil. The path was bordered by early tulips. But all these things were growing among as fine a crop of groundsel as Caroline had ever seen. For at least the whole of the spring the weeds had been allowed to have everything their own way and would soon be in complete mastery.

About the cottage itself there was the same air of recent neglect. The muslin curtains at the windows were dingy, but not yet downright dirty. Some amateurish patching had been done to the thatch. It all supported what Jan Pullen had told her about Jack Dawson. There was evidence here that for some time the people living in the cottage had fought a stubborn and on the whole successful battle with their discouraging conditions and had given in only a little while ago.

There was neither bell nor knocker on the door, so Caroline rapped on it with her knuckles.

When there was no answer, Mr. Sherwin, who had followed her up the path, gave a more peremptory knock. There was still silence inside, but after a moment the door of the next cottage opened and a big, slatternly woman looked out at them with an expression of rather contemptuous curiosity on her pale, fat face, as if she were mildly interested in knowing who could be so stupid as to knock at that door. But as soon as Mr. Sherwin started to speak to her, she retreated into her cottage, leaving the door only just open, so that she could go on peering out at them without being seen herself.

'Let's knock once more,' Caroline said, 'then if nothing happens I suppose we may as well go.'

He knocked again.

Still there was no sound of movement inside, but further up the row another door burst open and a small, intense-looking woman in an overall and bedroom slippers, with an old cardigan fastened across her chest with a safety pin, came running out. She started talking even before she reached her own gate.

'You won't find them, they've gone to their gran's, she come and took them, she come yesterday and she said to me, "Mrs. Pruitt," she said, "I'm taking them, it's what I should've done right at the beginning." "That's right," I said, "you should've done it long ago, Mrs. Dawson." She said to me, "Mrs. Pruitt," she said, "that's right, that's what I should've done, but you never can tell, can you?"'

By now the little woman had run in at the Dawsons' gate and was standing very close to Caroline and Mr. Sherwin, talking up into their faces.

'I said, "I could've told you, Mrs. Dawson",' she said. '"I could've told you it was what you'd have to do, unless you want them in a Home, because that's what it'll come to, it stands to reason," I said. "That's right," she said, "it stands to reason, but then I'm not young any more and I'm not one for interfering." "Mrs. Dawson," I said, "I know you never interfere, no more do I, as anyone will tell you, and I don't want you to think I've anything against Jack," I said, "he was a good boy till that woman got him, and if the worst happens, his death will be at her door, that's my opinion. But I'd have told you if you'd've

161

asked me, Mrs. Dawson," I said, "it's his character, you see, he'll never change it and you've got to think of the kids—"'

'Excuse me,' Mr. Sherwin interrupted, seeing that Mrs. Pruitt had such a miraculous control of her breathing that it appeared she would be able to talk on indefinitely without the slightest of pauses, 'do I understand that Mr. Dawson has had a serious accident?'

'Well!' she exclaimed, looking astonished and shocked by such ignorance. 'I thought it was what you come about. I thought you was from the Home. There was talk about sending them to the Home. That's why I said to you, "You won't find them, they've gone to their gran's," I said, "she come and took them—"'

'Mrs. Pruitt,' Mr. Sherwin cut in again swiftly, trying to prevent a repetition of the whole story, 'we came to talk to Mr. Dawson. We knew nothing about the accident. If you could tell us what happened—'

'Oh, you can't talk to him,' she said, 'not till Saturday.'

'Why not till Saturday?'

'Visiting time at the infirmary. Poor Jack, it's a shame, it wasn't none of his fault. That's what I said to his mother. "Mrs. Dawson," I said, "if the worst comes to the worst, it'll be at her door—"'

'Quite so, quite so, but how did it happen?' Mr. Sherwin insisted.

The answer came from the door of the next

162

cottage, where the big woman had reappeared and was standing, propping herself up slackly against the door post. 'Got stinking drunk, same as usual, drove head on into the vicar's car when it was standing in front of the church, cut his face, bust some ribs, but nobody's talking about him dying except Mrs. Know-All here.'

'What about the vicar?' Caroline asked with concern.

'Oh, he was doing a christening inside, he was all right,' the big woman said.

'Were there any witnesses to the accident?' Sherwin asked.

'Witnesses?' Mrs. Pruitt cried, while the big woman, who seemed to feel that there would be nothing more of interest in the conversation, heaved her massive body back into her cottage and slammed the door shut. 'Witnesses? The whole village. I saw it myself. I saw him coming just as I was crossing the road to the church, and I said to myself, I said . . .'

It was a difficult and time-consuming business trying to stop Mrs. Pruitt telling them what she had said to herself and to dislodge her from the gateway where, as they edged her down the path, she succeeded for some minutes in blocking their escape, but at last they gained the car.

As they drove off, Mr. Sherwin said, 'Well, what did you make of all that, Miss Dyer?'

Caroline gave an uncertain laugh. 'All I can think of at the moment is that, if you have to have an accident, you could hardly pick a more respectable way of having one than running into the vicar's car when it's standing still in front of the church, and hurting nobody but yourself.'

'Then you don't think Jack Dawson's a hired murderer? You don't think he's a member of a gang?'

The irony in his voice sparked off the anger that she had controlled earlier when he had tried to send her off to London.

'Even if he isn't, it doesn't mean there isn't a gang!' she said. 'It doesn't mean there wasn't meant to be a murder! We'd be fools to think so.'

He heard the change in her tone and adapted his own to it, speaking with quiet reasonableness. 'I dare say I am a fool, but I've got a feeling that your belief in this gang really all goes back to Lyddon's dramatics about his enemies and the rumour about the two strange men who've been around—whom you haven't seen yourself, however. If you could put them out of your mind and start again with just what you know of your own knowledge, I think you might come up with quite a different theory.'

'Do you mean you don't believe in those men?' she asked.

'Oh, I believe they exist,' he said. 'I believe they came around asking questions of some sort. But I believe it was probably Lyddon's dramatics about them that first upset your sister and sent her rushing off to get hold of you—which is what happened, isn't it? I believe there's a good chance that there's nothing any more sinister about them than about Jack Dawson.'

'But you said yourself there was something awfully wrong about the fire last night,' she reminded him. '*Another* fire, you said, caused by defective wiring, as if you didn't think it could possibly be a coincidence.'

She saw the colour suddenly deepen in his cheeks. 'Did I? Yes, I know I did. I'm sorry, I wish I hadn't. As you said, I think, I'm over-sensitive on the subject of fires. And I was hoping—I realise I couldn't have chosen a more foolish method—that I could persuade you to go back to London. But you're remembering you've promised to think about going, aren't you?'

She noticed the change of subject, as well as having noticed, she thought, a lack of candour in his voice. So he did not mean to let her know what he thought had been so awfully wrong with the fire. She shrugged her shoulders and said that perhaps she might think of going home tomorrow or the day after, depending on what Harry and Fenella felt about it.

But even if she had wanted to find out what Harry and Fenella felt about it, the chance to discuss it, or anything else of any moment, did not come that day. There was too much coming and going in the house. The village builder spent several hours with Harry, while Fenella for once cooked lunch, producing tinned pea soup and warmed-up frozen fish cakes and chips and a glutinous white pudding that came out of a packet. When Harry discovered what she had prepared, he refused to eat it, demanding bread and cheese instead. He was abrupt and rude. Caroline half-expected Fenella to fly into one of her hysterical rages, but instead of looking hurt, or even irritated, she looked humble and loving and eager to please him. Meeting Caroline's eyes briefly across the table, she gave an apologetic smile. As plainly as words, it asked that Caroline should forget everything that Fenella had said to her about Harry, for difficult as he might be, she was proud of him, loved him, and was going to learn to put up with him, whatever it cost her.

Emma Dewhurst watched Harry with almost the same expression of love on her face. Her eyes followed him about the room and she looked forlorn when he hurried out, which he did as soon as he could. Having so much tenderness and admiration lavished on him seemed quite to destroy his self-confidence. He was more ill at ease than Caroline had ever seen him.

He went out into the garden to talk to Jan

Pullen, who had just arrived with the new car that Caroline had heard Harry talking about earlier on the telephone. She could see the two men through the window, quite amicably discussing the car. Then they got into it and drove off together.

Mrs. Dewhurst gave a soft sigh and turned to Fenella.

'You know, dear, there's something I feel I must say to you,' she said. 'I'd like to say it to your dear Harry too, but I know it would only embarrass him. They do get embarrassed so easily by a little show of feeling, don't they? Men, I mean. Well, dear, it's just that I don't think I've been nearly grateful enough to you both for all you've done for me these last six months. No—' She raised her voice a little as Fenella tried to interrupt her. 'I mean it. I've been so dull and sorry for myself and not thinking at all what it must be like for young people like you to have someone like me around. I've even, I'm sorry to say, been quite irritated sometimes with the heedless way Harry talks, as if he didn't realise—as if he never thought . . .'

Her voice was threatening to become tearful. She paused a moment and somehow managed to make her writhing little red mouth grow firm in a determined smile.

'I didn't mean to say that,' she proceeded. 'I know he's only joking and of course never thinks of one's overhearing him, so it isn't meant to hurt one. It's just that when he thinks it's so funny to say I poisoned my darling husband, when I remember how terribly he suffered, that I can't quite bear . . .'

The smile had slipped. She snatched a lacy handkerchief out of the sleeve of her emerald green jersey dress and dabbed at her overflowing eyes.

'No, that isn't what I meant to say,' she said. 'I must stop feeling sorry for myself. There are lots of other people who are alone in the world and they haven't been so wonderfully taken care of as I have—and more than that, so much more. I just can't get the words out, dear, but last night was such a lesson. I'll never forget it. Such selflessness, such heroism . . .'

Fenella's eyes were swimming too by then. She reached out a hand to Mrs. Dewhurst, who clasped it eagerly. As they both gave themselves up happily to their emotions Caroline left them.

She went up to her room, took off her dress, put on her dressing-gown and lay down on the bed.

She intended to think right back to the beginning of all the puzzling and worrying things that had happened, starting with the day when Harry had dropped his first facetious hints to her about the fire in the bookshop, about the manner of Mr. Dewhurst's death, about Jan Pullen. Then she would try to make up her mind how many of them were truly strange and truly worrying, and how many of them only seemed so because of the nonsense that Harry had woven around them. But the trouble was that as soon as she lay down, she did not want to think at all, but only to shut her eyes, to rest, to sleep. She had not realised how exhausted she was, how impossible it was suddenly going to feel to keep going any longer.

For the first time she thought that Hugh Sherwin's attempt to make her go home had been wholly wise and kind and that she ought to have listened to him. It would be wonderful to be back in her flat now, hearing the familiar, unintrusive rumble of the traffic, the quacking sound of the next-door radio that had so often irritated her, the chirping of the London sparrows in the big plane tree in the garden, and to know that nobody could suddenly walk into the flat and wake her up against her will, that nobody was even going to want to do so and come knocking at her door—knock, knock, knock, insistent and yet somehow furtive, so that she had to struggle back from the calms of sleep, force her eyes to open and call out, 'Come in!'

The door opened softly and Mrs. Dewhurst sidled in, closed it as carefully as if she were afraid of waking Caroline and came tip-toeing across the room towards her.

'You aren't asleep?' she whispered. 'I was so afraid perhaps I'd be disturbing you. But I must talk to someone. I need advice so badly. Do you mind? Will you let me talk to you for just a few minutes?'

'Of course,' Caroline answered, and only when she had said it wondered why she had whispered too. Deliberately raising her voice to its normal pitch, she repeated, 'Yes, of course. Pull up that chair and sit down.'

Mrs. Dewhurst started as if Caroline had suddenly bellowed at her. She looked round nervously, drew up a chair and sat down on the edge of it. She leant towards Caroline, so that Caroline caught the scent of the powder and cream on her face.

In the same whisper as before, Mrs. Dewhurst said, 'I know you need to rest, so I promise I shan't be long, but I'm so torn with doubt and uncertainty, I don't know what to do. And for all I know, it's already too late to do anything. I expect I ought to have spoken out at once, and not worried about the consequences. If you stick to the truth, you can't go far wrong, can you? Well, that's what people say . . . But there's gratitude to be considered too. Perhaps it matters as much as truth. What do you think, dear?'

'Gratitude?' Caroline said, again finding her voice infected by Mrs. Dewhurst's whispering. 'To Harry, do you mean?'

Mrs. Dewhurst nodded her head earnestly. 'I owe him so much. I don't have to tell you. You saw it. And I mean it when I say I'd do

170

anything for him and for your dear sister. I mean every word. But perhaps not telling the truth isn't really helping them, that's what's worrying me, you see. Perhaps it'll actually turn out to be the worst thing I could have done for them.'

Caroline sat up in bed and swung her feet to the floor.

In great agitation Mrs. Dewhurst exclaimed, 'Oh, I *have* disturbed you! I'm so sorry, I know I oughtn't to have come. But I'm not used to making up my own mind about important things, and I feel this is terribly important.'

'I expect it is,' Caroline said. She stood up and started wandering about the room, looking for her cigarettes. 'It's something to do with that man you heard in the house last night, is it?'

'That man?' Mrs. Dewhurst said in a tone of surprise. 'Oh no, dear, I've told the police everything I know about him. It isn't much, of course, and there's a lot about it I don't understand at all, like my clothes and things being thrown out of the window. I suppose I must have done that myself, though I can't remember anything about it. But the doctor told me it's quite easy to forget everything you did just before getting a blow on the head and that probably I did it when I first smelt the fire and before I went along the passage and perhaps fell and hit my head on the chest there. I don't know. I think—I'm sure—I

171

heard someone downstairs, but no one seems to think I could have.'

'I think you could have,' Caroline said. 'I think you did.'

Beyond the flame of the match that she had just struck to light her cigarette she saw Mrs. Dewhurst's round, watery eyes turn glassy and blank. She put a hand to her mouth.

'Oh dear,' she mumbled behind her fingers, 'oh dear, what shall I do?'

'Have you told the police there's someone you're afraid of?' Caroline asked. 'Someone you think might have come after you?'

'Afraid of?' The glassiness of Mrs. Dewhurst's eyes had fixed a look of frightened surprise on her face. 'Me? But I'm not afraid of anyone. Not for myself. Good gracious, why ever should I be?'

'I don't know. But don't you remember asking me if I was wearing my blue coat when the van hit Harry's car? Didn't that mean you were afraid that I'd been mistaken for you, because you've got a blue coat yourself and we've both got dark hair?'

Mrs. Dewhurst's hand went self-consciously to her dyed black hair.

'Oh no, dear, I wasn't thinking of myself,' she said. 'I was thinking of your sister. She's got a blue coat too.'

'Fenella? I haven't seen it,' Caroline said.

'No, I don't think she's worn it for some time. I think it's more a real winter coat and too heavy for this time of year.'

'In that case you were afraid someone wanted to kill Fenella.'

'Fenella—and Harry.'

They stared at one another.

Then, doing her best to keep her voice normal, Caroline asked, 'What made you think that, Mrs. Dewhurst?'

'Emma—do call me Emma, dear.'

'Emma.'

'Well, all sorts of little things have been happening, like that man coming here, asking questions. I know Fenella got badly frightened by that. I was in the house, you see. I heard some of it. But perhaps it was really just the way Harry talked. I think I was expecting something awful to happen. Of course, by now I know that three-quarters of what he says is nonsense, but at first I believed it all and so I'm really in an awful muddle about what I thought—because I'm not very quick and even now I generally start by believing he's serious and I have to notice that other people don't before I'm sure he isn't. But this isn't what I wanted your advice about. I'd never have disturbed you just for this. It's about the reading-lamp.'

'The reading-lamp?'

'The one that started the fire. So they say.'

'So *who* say?'

'Everyone,' Mrs. Dewhurst breathed almost inaudibly. 'Harry told them the flex on the reading-lamp was very old and they all said that explained it. The insulation had broken down, they said, and the thing started sparking. And I haven't contradicted them, I've let it pass. And that's what I'm so worried about now. At first I did it because I was too dazed to realise what was being said. Then, when I began to understand, I thought I mustn't say anything in case it affects the insurance or something—I know so little about that sort of thing. But at least I felt sure I owed it to Harry not to say anything about the lamp that he didn't say himself. I didn't actually have to lie, you see. I only had to say nothing. But now I don't know, I don't know!' She rocked backwards and forwards on the edge of her chair. 'Suppose they're in danger, those two, suppose there *was* a man in the house last night, and suppose something awful happens just because I never told the police that really there wasn't anything wrong with the lamp.'

'How do you know there wasn't anything wrong with the lamp?' Caroline asked.

'Because Fenella mended it only a week or two ago. *I* saw her. You know how clever she is about mechanical things. Well, she removed the old flex and put on a new one, all shiny in a plastic cover. And she tested it and everything was perfect.'

Caroline sat down abruptly on the edge of the bed.

'Oh God, the fools!' she said. 'Why couldn't

174

they simply say so?'

'I know,' Mrs. Dewhurst said. 'But now the question is, what ought I to do? It isn't that I mind admitting to the police that I didn't tell them the whole truth before, it's just that—just that I can't face telling them that Harry and Fenella deliberately lied to them about the lamp. Because that's what it comes to, doesn't it? They told a deliberate lie.'

'At least Fenella did,' Caroline said. 'Are you sure Harry knew the lamp had been mended?'

Mrs. Dewhurst thought it over. 'Not absolutely *sure*,' she said. 'I just took it for granted.'

Caroline nodded. 'Thank you for telling me about this,' she said. 'If you don't mind, I'd like to think it over before we decide to do anything.'

'Of course, dear,' Mrs. Dewhurst said. 'That's what I expected. I wasn't thinking of rushing off to the police straight away, I just wanted the help of someone with a better head than mine. I feel much better already, now that I've told you about it, and I'm quite ready to follow your advice, whatever it is. If you tell me to say nothing about the lamp, I shan't say anything. And there's always the chance, I suppose, that there was something else wrong with it besides the flex, or even that Fenella got the wires mixed up or something. So now lie down again and have a nice rest. I shan't disturb you any more.'

175

She got up and tip-toed out of the room.

However, for Caroline to rest any longer was something that Mrs. Dewhurst had made quite impossible. Fenella, Caroline knew, did not get wires mixed up, did not make blunders when she had a screwdriver in those slender, useless-looking hands. If she had set out to mend the lamp, it would have been as good as new when she had finished with it. Exceedingly dismayed by Mrs. Dewhurst's story, Caroline got dressed again and went downstairs to look for Fenella.

She was in the dining-room with Harry and Jan Pullen. They were sitting round the fire with drinks and talking about cars. Harry had decided to buy the one that Jan had been demonstrating to him. They made room for Caroline by the fire and Harry brought her a drink. For the next hour they sat and talked about cars, nothing but cars. The manner of the two men was friendly and practical. Fenella, who sat with her dreamy eyes on Harry's face and her slim body relaxed in a deep chair, might not have existed.

Yet she was looking unusually lovely that evening, and she had dressed for the occasion too. For to her it was an occasion, Caroline perceived, perhaps as important as any in her life. She had put on a full-skirted dress of a dark material that had a metallic thread woven through it, which shone bronze in the firelight, and she had put up her hair, brushing it back

176

from her face in a smooth sweep which made her look, it struck Caroline all of a sudden, far more exposed than usual. Fenella had so often used her heavy curtain of hair as a concealment, had so often retreated behind it. But now it was as if she had at last made up her mind that she loved her husband and that she wanted him to see it.

It might have been because he did see it, and because Jan saw it too, that both of them were so careful hardly to glance in her direction. Presently they went out together to take another look at the car, but by then Mr. Sherwin had joined them and Caroline had no opportunity to talk to Fenella. After a few minutes they heard Jan drive away and Harry come in alone and go to the kitchen. Fenella waited for a little while, talking disconnectedly with her thoughts obviously far away, then she got up and drifted out to join him.

Dinner was very late that evening, although it was only soup, omelettes and cheese. It was a silent meal and although Fenella's face was unusually serene, Harry was still too subdued to seem quite himself. Everyone was very tired and went early to bed.

But that was no help at all, so far as Caroline was concerned. She was feeling more and more worried by a phrase that Mrs. Dewhurst had let fall, 'Suppose it affects the insurance or something . . .'

Caroline thought of Fenella tinkering with

177

the lamp. She thought of the way they had all gone out that evening. But in the end they had had to leave Mrs. Dewhurst behind and surely they wouldn't have done that if they had known that the house was going to catch fire. All the same, it seemed to account for Harry's mood more convincingly than anything else. He would always be subdued by failure . . .

When Caroline turned out her light, Jan Pullen was already at his mysterious hammering and that night he kept it up for hours. It seemed even louder than usual too, even angrier. To begin with Caroline felt quite ready to pity him because of the way that Fenella had shown him her feelings that evening, but after a while she thought that she would pity him far more wholeheartedly if he would release his jealousy and disappointment in a way less upsetting to everyone else. There were streaks of daylight in the sky before he stopped and she at last fell asleep.

She awoke to nightmare. Fenella was in her room, shaking her and sobbing.

'He's dead!' she screamed in Caroline's ear. 'He's been killed—wake up Caroline!—he took the new car out and smashed it up! Harry's dead!'

178

CHAPTER THIRTEEN

Caroline tumbled out of bed. Grabbing her dressing-gown, she fumbled her way into the sleeves. She was still half-blind with sleep and hardly knew what she was doing.

Fenella had collapsed on the bed. Her face was buried in the pillow and she was moaning into it. For the moment Caroline left her there and ran out into the passage.

Sergeant Rutter and Hugh Sherwin were at the bottom of the stairs. Both men looked up at her when she appeared on the stairs above them, but neither of them wanted to speak. Each left it to the other.

Going down to them, she asked, 'Is it true?'

They both nodded.

Mr. Sherwin added in a strained voice, 'Lyddon took the new car out. He got to the top of the cutting all right, then something seems to have gone wrong. Going down the hill, he lost control and crashed head on into the wall of Pullen's garage. He was killed on the spot.'

'How long ago?' she asked.

'About half an hour. Pullen got the police at once and Sergeant Rutter came up to break the news to Mrs. Lyddon.'

'So Harry was right all the time, someone wanted to kill him.'

If Caroline had been capable of thinking, she would not have said it. But just then there did not seem to be anything else worth saying. She turned and started up the stairs again. Sergeant Rutter took a quick step after her.

'Excuse me, Miss Dyer—'

'Not now,' she said and went on up the stairs. 'I must get back to my sister.'

'Just one moment,' Mr. Sherwin said quietly. 'I think you'll have to tell the sergeant what you meant by that.'

She stood still almost at the top of the stairs. Looking down, she was puzzled by the change on Sergeant Rutter's face. She had quite forgotten that when she had stated that someone had wanted to kill Harry, she had spoken aloud.

'Who did Mr. Lyddon think wanted to kill him, Miss Dyer?' the sergeant asked.

'He didn't know, or he didn't want us to think he did,' she said. 'But he believed that accident we were in, he and I, was supposed to get rid of him. I didn't think so. I thought—at least, yesterday I thought . . .' She put her hands to her head. She had almost said that yesterday she had thought that it was Emma Dewhurst whom someone wanted to kill. But now she did not know if she thought that any longer. 'I thought it was all imagination,' she said. 'But there've been two men round the place, strange men no one knew anything about. Mr. Lyddon was worried about them.

Mr. Sherwin can tell you about that. I really must get back to my sister.'

She went quickly back to her room.

Fenella was just where Caroline had left her, lying across the bed with her face hidden in the pillow and her arms flung wide. She looked as limp as if she had just fallen there, but Caroline noticed that her hands were clenched.

She bent over her and touched her on the shoulder. 'Fenella—'

Fenella moved her head a little on the pillow so that she could speak.

'Have you ever felt like a murderess?' she asked.

'Why?' Caroline's voice sounded strange to her, thin and sharp and not at all as she had intended.

'It's how I feel.'

'Don't say things like that,' Caroline said. 'They won't help. They aren't true.'

'Yes, it's true.'

'You don't know anything about how this happened.'

'No, but I . . .' Fenella gave a deep sigh and sat up. Her hair streamed loosely round her blotchy face. 'I wanted it to happen, Caroline. Deep inside me it's what I really wanted.'

'You didn't!' Caroline no longer cared how sharp her voice sounded. 'You're feeling guilty because somehow or other you didn't manage to save him. Everyone feels that when someone dies. There's always a feeling that if only one had somehow been able to give more, they'd have lived.'

'No,' Fenella said, 'I wanted to be free.'

'You didn't,' Caroline repeated. 'Oh, sometimes, I dare say. But not really. Not last night, for instance.'

'Last night doesn't count,' Fenella said.

'Why not?'

'I was in a sort of dream. It wouldn't have lasted.'

'You may find it's one of the only nights that does count.'

Fenella shook her head in a gesture of unspeakable weariness. 'It's something you'd never understand.'

'But however mixed up you've been about Harry,' Caroline said, 'it had nothing to do with his smashing himself up in his car.'

'What do you know about it?'

Fenella's tone was flat and cold. Her face was slack and empty. It frightened Caroline. Despair, the kind that truly rejects all hope and all help, would look like that, she thought.

'Have you had any breakfast?' As soon as she had said it, Caroline felt shocked by the banality of the question. Yet wasn't it commonsense that the effects of disaster must be at their most devastating on an empty stomach? Thank God for commonsense, which bridges the too terrifying chasms of emotion.

'Yes, but you haven't,' Fenella said. She stood up unsteadily. 'I'll go down and see to it.'

'I'll see to it,' Caroline said. 'You stay here. I'll bring up some coffee.'

'No.' Shaking off Caroline's hand, Fenella took a few steps towards the door. 'I'll go. I can't stay here, they'll want me.'

'The police?'

Fenella did not answer, and at the first step she took, dumped to the floor in a dead faint.

Caroline ran out into the passage. She called Hugh Sherwin and he and Sergeant Rutter came up together, carried Fenella to her room and laid her on the bed. She was not unconscious for long, but when she opened her eyes again she seemed not to know where she was, or what had happened. She seemed surprised to see Caroline standing there and asked her vaguely when she had arrived. Yet when Caroline was going to leave the room to tell Mr. Sherwin to telephone for the doctor, Fenella caught hold of her wrist with that surprising strength of hers and would not let her go.

Mr. Sherwin had already telephoned for the doctor. Mrs. Dewhurst came tip-toeing into the room to tell Caroline so. Mrs. Dewhurst had already changed into black, but unfortunately it only made her look as if she were ready to go out for cocktails.

Putting her lips close to Caroline's ear, she whispered, 'There are some more policemen downstairs now, dear, and one of them, an inspector, I think, asked to see you. I'll sit with Fenella while you're gone.'

Somehow Caroline unwound Fenella's fingers from her wrist and went out, leaving Mrs. Dewhurst sitting on a chair at the bedside.

Caroline went back to her room, dressed and went downstairs.

She found Detective-Inspector Ingram wandering about the house, interestedly examining the results of the fire. He was very willing to join her for a cup of coffee in the comparatively draught-free kitchen. He was a big man, burly and in a meaty way, quite handsome. In the right uniform, with enough gold braid, he would have made a very impressive commissionaire. At the same time, there was plenty of intelligence in his heavy face and his blue eyes were keen and watchful.

He said very little until the coffee had been made and they were both seated facing each other across the plastic-topped table. Then he started abruptly, 'Now about what you told Sergeant Rutter, Miss Dyer. You told him Mr. Lyddon thought someone wanted to kill him. You said something about two strange men. Will you tell me what you meant?'

Sipping the hot coffee, Caroline found her thoughts straying helplessly. She hardly knew what she had meant. And she had started to think about food. It was not because she was in the least hungry, but it had just occurred to her that with Harry dead and Fenella in a state of collapse, she would have to do the cooking, and although she was not a very competent cook, the thought of having something practical to do was so steadying that she did not want to let go of it.

'Did someone kill him?' she asked, concentrating hard on the problem of what she would cook for lunch. It helped amazingly to keep her voice level, if not to clear her mind. 'Was it murder?'

'I'm afraid that's going too fast for me,' the inspector said. 'I've only just started trying to find out what happened. But you said that Mr. Lyddon thought someone wanted to kill him.'

She thought, 'It ought to be something very plain, like boiled fish with parsley sauce.' But that took her straight back to her week in the hospital. A good steak was really a much better idea, if there was such a thing in the house, which there probably wasn't.

'I suppose you know all about the accident he and I were in a few days ago,' she said.

'I've been told about it, yes.'

'Well, Mr. Lyddon seemed sure we'd been run into on purpose,' she said. 'He talked about knowing too much about certain people and said they'd come after him.'

'He didn't say what people?'

'No, and none of us took him seriously. He always dramatised things a great deal. But then we had the fire, so I began to wonder . . .'

'He wasn't in the house at the time, was he?'

'No, there was no one here but Mrs. Dewhurst. And Harry had told us that he'd got written records of everything he knew about these people, whoever they are, put away somewhere safe, so that there wasn't any point in killing him . . . As I said, we didn't take any of it seriously. But the fire seems to have started in the room where anyone would suppose he kept his records. His desk and his files were quite burnt up. And now that he's been killed . . .' She frowned in confusion. 'I don't know what it all means. I don't know what I meant by what I said to Sergeant Rutter. I'm sorry.'

'What did Mr. Lyddon say about the fire?' Ingram asked. 'Did he accuse the same people of having started it, or anything like that?'

'That was the queer thing about it,' Caroline said, 'he didn't. When I suggested it, he only said he'd been talking nonsense the other evening and that if I knew him better, I'd have realised he often did that and that I shouldn't have taken any notice of him.'

'And that worried you?' Ingram said.

'Very much.'

'Why?'

'It was so unlike him. Something queer seemed to have happened to him. He seemed . . . It's difficult to explain, because the one thing I'm quite sure of is that he was an awfully brave man, but it was as if he'd suddenly got deadly scared of something.'

'Brave people aren't immune from getting deadly scared,' he said.

'All the same, it was terribly puzzling.' She reached for his cup to refill it. 'He got so subdued, it was as if he was thinking hard all the time about something very worrying, yet he insisted there wouldn't have been any point in destroying his records, which were only notes and newspaper cuttings, when all he'd have to do was write them out again. But now, you see . . .'

'Hm, yes, only now he can't.' He put several spoonfuls of sugar into his coffee. 'I suppose he didn't write them out again—yesterday, I mean, after the fire.'

'I don't know,' Caroline said. 'But from something he said, I'm inclined to think they hadn't been destroyed. He said to me, "I've got a lot of notes and cuttings, but of course they aren't quite the dynamite I tried to make out." Speaking in the present tense, you see, as if the things still existed.'

Ingram stroked one of his smooth, ruddy cheeks. 'Of course, it could have been a slip of the tongue.'

'But he could have meant it.'

'And you think he meant it. It's certainly an interesting point. Now about the two men who were here . . .'

Caroline told him what she knew of them

and for the first time since he had started questioning her, Ingram made notes of her answers.

'Now about the car,' he said. 'This new car. Do you know where it was left during the night?'

'I imagine Harry put it into the garage,' she said.

'Aren't you certain?'

She shook her head. 'The last I saw of it was at the front door. My brother-in-law and Mr. Pullen had come back from their trial run together and came in for a drink. I don't remember hearing Harry put it away.'

'So you don't know if anyone could have got at it during the night.'

'Oh, even if it was put in the garage, that wouldn't have made any difference. The garage was hardly ever locked. If the car was tampered with . . .' She paused. '*Was* the car tampered with, Inspector?'

He answered cautiously. 'At the moment I'm only assuming that that isn't impossible. It was a brand new car, it had behaved satisfactorily during the afternoon, then something went wrong with the steering, extremely wrong. That's all we know. But you'd started to say something, Miss Dyer.'

'I was only going to say that if the car was tampered with during the night, it could have been done even more easily in the garage than out in the drive, because we shouldn't have heard anything.'

'No, or seen a light. He must have used a light, I think.'

'Was it a skilled bit of work?' she asked.

'Quite skilled, I should imagine. If, you understand, it wasn't an accident. That still isn't impossible.' He stood up. 'But a lot of people know about cars these days. You don't have to be in the trade. Do you think Mrs. Lyddon would know where the car was left for the night?'

'She might, but I don't think you'll be able to talk to her yet.'

In fact, the doctor would not let Fenella answer any questions till the afternoon. Until then, Caroline and Mrs. Dewhurst took it in turns to sit with her. About mid-day Jan Pullen came up to the house to ask how she was, but she refused to see him, refused swiftly and with a shudder that shook her from head to foot. Then, as if to cover this, she said that she couldn't see anybody, anybody at all.

'I don't mean you,' she added, looking up rather vacantly at her sister, and whenever Caroline tried to leave the room, she clung to her, saying that it scared her to be left alone and that Caroline was the only person whom she could trust now.

'Harry cured me of trusting people,' she said, still with the flat note of despair in her voice that Caroline found far more harrowing than her floods of tears, 'because I couldn't trust him. I wanted to—I tried—but I couldn't. And d'you know something, Caroline? That's driven me nearly mad. Oh yes, I don't think I've been quite sane for some time.'

Sitting by the bed, letting Fenella keep a tight hold of her hand in a way that made the years slip away and Fenella seem almost the child again who at that time perhaps had really trusted her sister, Caroline wondered if it had been her fault that Fenella had grown up into this woman who, except on the surface, was incapable of trusting any of the people who were nearest to her. To be loved by Fenella was to be feared and suspected by her.

Lunch, after all, was not cooked by Caroline, but by Mrs. Freely, who got busy with a tin-opener, so that the household did not go hungry. But in the afternoon, when the police were at last allowed to see Fenella, and Inspector Ingram made it plain that he wanted to see her alone, Caroline was glad to escape from the bedroom to the kitchen. All of a sudden it had become unbearable to her to go on being as idle as she had been for the last fortnight. If she could not find something useful to do, she might soon be as near the edge of insanity as Fenella had claimed to be.

But unfortunately, Caroline was not a knowledgeable cook. Living alone, she had always concentrated on the quick and the simple. Yet what she wanted now was something that would take the long hours of the whole afternoon to prepare and to watch over. So when she had investigated the refrigerator and the pantry, she looked round for a cookery book to see if it would give her inspiration.

She soon found, not one cookery book, but about fifty on a shelf in a cupboard. There was Mrs. Beeton at one end and Fanny Farmer at the other, and in between were books of French, German, Italian, Hungarian and Chinese recipes, and many more. The profusion was almost too much for her. Picking out one book at random, she started reading, then went on to another, then another, and in a little while had that feeling of indigestion which is easily induced by a too intensive reading of cookery books. She had begun to think that perhaps she would settle for shepherd's pie after all, which she could cook without instructions, when she noticed a loose-leaf notebook tucked in amongst the rest. She took it out and turned the pages curiously.

This, she found, was where Harry had written down recipes that apparently had particularly pleased him. Also he had pasted in some that he had cut from newspapers and magazines. In the margins beside some of these he had scribbled notes, mostly corrections of quantities, of oven temperatures or of the time of cooking. As Caroline flipped over the pages, her eye was caught by a recipe for cold cucumber soup, then by one for profiteroles with hot chocolate sauce, then, all of a sudden, by a headline at which she stared for a moment in wonder. What was it doing in a cookery book? *'Arsenic in the Cocoa.'*

Under it she read, 'The body of the woman who was found dead in a pond near Knaresborough on Wednesday has been identified as that of Mrs. Laura Belper Dewbury (59), widow of Mr. Sidney Belper Dewbury, who died a week ago as the result of swallowing arsenic in a cup of cocoa. The body was identified by her son, Mr. Mervyn Dewbury, who said his mother had been much depressed since the death of her husband and had several times threatened to take her life. Her death was due to drowning.'

Beside this clipping, Harry had put an exclamation mark.

Caroline's hands had started to shake. By chance, she realised, she had stumbled on Harry's records.

CHAPTER FOURTEEN

Absorbed, Caroline went on turning the pages. Pasted in alongside recipes for salads and sauces, for *coq au vin* and *rum baba*, she found accounts of robberies and rapes, of embezzlements and murders. Most of them were tantalisingly incomplete and Harry's notes in the margins made them no clearer. One or two pages were entirely in Harry's handwriting. These, she guessed, were stories that had never been printed. She was working her way through one of these, not too easily, because it was written in a small, fluid scribble, when Hugh Sherwin came in and found her at it.

Excitedly she handed the notebook to him.

'Look,' she said, 'read that.'

He thought that she was pointing at a recipe for eel pie.

'No,' he said positively. 'There might be times when I could look that in the face, but not today.'

'No, the one beside it,' Caroline said.

He read the first few words aloud. ' "The Brig. sentenced yesterday—only five years . . ." ' He broke off with a startled exclamation, and as Caroline had done, quickly turned the pages. 'Harry's records,' he said. 'His notes and cuttings.'

'Yes, but go on reading the one about the Brig.,' she said. 'It's interesting.'

He turned back to the page that she had first shown him and with a deepening frown started reading it to her again.

' "The Brig. sentenced yesterday—only five years, because first offence(!) I went back to the garage today, talked to neighbours. Indignation that he didn't get ten. Are as anti him now as they were pro before trial. Every car theft in country blamed on him. All remember things they denied beforehand, strange noises at night, strange men hanging around, no one said, 'Such a nice fellow, well educated too, can't believe anything against him.' They jeer at the police for having taken so long to get on his trail, ask why they haven't found the money he salted away, why they haven't rounded up rest of gang. Feel they've been made fools of, hostility in proportion to degree they were impressed before. Or is it effect of real wife turning up at trial? The blonde has discreetly vanished, as blondes do. No one with good word for her, instead of 'real lady,' etc. Short story?"'

'Well?' Caroline said when Mr. Sherwin stopped.

'It's the story Lyddon told us the other morning, isn't it?' he said. 'The one about the man who used to buy up badly damaged cars very cheap and transfer the registration and so on to a stolen car of the same make and year, then sell the stolen car as a brilliant repair job. It's dated just over two years ago.'

'Yes—and now look at this one.' Caroline turned the pages back to the first that had caught her eye.

He read the story of the acquittal of Mrs. Laura Belper Dewbury.

When he had finished it, he gave a short laugh. 'Dewbury—Dewhurst,' he muttered.

'What do you make of that?'

'I don't know.'

'Lyddon may have made these notes in the first place because he thought he could use them in his writing.' He handed the notebook back to Caroline. 'Just notes for possible stories. Which might be why he said they weren't dynamite.'

'Yet he hid them rather carefully, didn't he?' She showed him where she had found the notebook. 'Who'd think of looking for things like this among his cookery books?'

He read the titles, took out one or two of the books, glanced through them and put them back on the shelf.

'I'd say the question is, did he hide them at all?' he said. 'Isn't this just where he pasted in any odd thing that happened to interest him?'

'The things that interested him being cooking and crime?'

'Well, weren't they? He'd been a crime reporter and he'd become a cook.'

'And he was murdered. And I'll tell you something else. Fenella's been very worried because he always had money that she couldn't account for.' She closed the cupboard door on Harry's cookery books, sat down at the table and opened the loose-leaf notebook again. 'No, I'm sure this was a hiding-place of something he thought really was dynamite. That's why he started saying it wasn't. He'd been frightened by something that happened

195

on the night of the fire and he started trying to spread the idea around that he didn't know anything important about anyone at all. But he was too late.'

Mr. Sherwin stood looking at her thoughtfully for a moment. His eyes, behind the thick spectacles, were narrowed in concentration.

'Miss Dyer, have you thought how many people heard Lyddon say he had those records?' he asked.

'How can we tell?' she replied.

'There were just you and I and your sister and Mrs. Dewhurst in the room.'

'But probably that wasn't the only time he talked like that,' she said. 'Lots of other people may have heard him.'

'Pullen, for instance?'

'Yes, for one.'

'You haven't made up your mind Pullen killed him, his friend Jack Dawson having failed?'

'Well, look at this story about the character he calls the Brig.,' she said. 'The Brig. must be in prison still, if he got five years, but it says here they never rounded up the rest of the gang. If Jan belonged to it, if he was carrying on the same trade here and if Harry found out, that could explain a good deal.'

'Except why Pullen decided to do a murder in a way that was bound to make him chief suspect.'

'Perhaps he couldn't think of any other way.'

'Somehow I think he's more intelligent than that,' Mr. Sherwin said.

'But he had to be quick, don't you see? Assuming he believed he'd managed to destroy Harry's records in the fire, he'd have known he'd got to act fast, or Harry could have written everything out again.'

'Oh, Pullen set the house on fire too, did he? He's been busy lately.'

Caroline's hands tightened on the notebook. She felt a very strong impulse to throw it straight in his face. It was beginning to infuriate her that he would not take any of her ideas seriously. Yesterday he had refused to believe that the fire had been anything but an accident, that Mrs. Dewhurst had heard any footsteps in the house or seen any strange man. Today he would not even consider the possibility that Jan Pullen was a member of a gang of car-thieves. And, of all things, he appeared to want Caroline to believe that the notes which Harry had hidden so cunningly had been meant only for the stories he might some day have written. It was almost as if Mr. Sherwin felt that she was trying to dramatise things in the same way as Harry and had to be discouraged.

'I don't know why you won't listen to anything I say,' she said, 'unless there's something you know about all this that I don't.'

She saw a spark of anger in his eyes, but when he answered, his voice was even quieter than usual and almost prim in its deliberation.

'I believe I can say quite accurately that I've no knowledge that you haven't, Miss Dyer,' he said, 'except for one thing. I know whether or not I set my shop on fire. You may believe me that I didn't, or you may believe I did, but you can't *know*. Concerning everything else that's happened in the last few days, however, we start equal, and what strikes me most about the little that we know is that we'd be most ill-advised to leap to any hasty conclusions. So let me point out certain things about this notebook before you start building too much on what you may find in it. Take the story of Mrs. Laura Belper Dewbury. Remember that it amused your brother-in-law to suggest to people that our Mrs. Dewhurst poisoned her husband by giving him arsenic in a cup of cocoa. Very well, why not decide that she's really Mrs. Dewbury and that the dead woman who was identified as Mrs. Dewbury was really someone else? Why not decide that Lyddon knew this, was blackmailing her and that she murdered him to get free of his power over her? Have you decided this? Perhaps you have.'

Caroline stirred uneasily. 'I haven't really thought—'

He broke in, 'There's probably a very simple reason why you haven't. It's that the age of Mrs. Dewbury is given here as fifty-nine. And this cutting isn't new, so if she's still alive, she's even older than that. And I think you'll agree with me that even if Emma Dewhurst's raven hair is snow-white under the dye, she can't be much more than fifty.'

'There are other reasons too,' Caroline said. 'Inspector Ingram says this murderer must be a skilled mechanic.'

'In fact, it's only the coincidence of the names that's in any way interesting,' Mr. Sherwin said. 'So you see where that leaves you.'

'You think it's the coincidence of the names that put the idea in Harry's head, that it was that that made him think of tormenting her in that particular way?'

She thought that he hesitated before he answered, as if he had lost the thread of his argument. When he spoke, it was without the note of prickly anger. 'Well, she can't be Mrs. Dewbury, can she? Allowing for all the miracles of science, can our Emma be, say, sixty-one?'

She smiled. 'No.'

'So there you are.'

'And you don't think we ought to do anything about this notebook?'

'Not at all, we must give it to the police.'

'But if it's all nonsense . . .'

'They're the people to decide if it is or not.'

She pushed the book across the table

towards him. 'Will you see about it then? I'm going to make a shepherd's pie for dinner.'

If the meal that Caroline eventually produced was not worthy of Harry, it could have been worse, she thought, very much worse, although so little was eaten that it looked as if no one quite agreed with her. Mrs. Dewhurst only pecked at what was on her plate. Caroline herself started well, but soon had to give up. Hugh Sherwin went on doggedly until he had finished what she had given him, but she thought that this was more from a determination not to hurt her feelings than from appetite.

Fenella ate nothing at all. She had stayed in her room all day, lying on her bed or sitting in a chair by the fire, sometimes crying violently, sometimes staring blankly into space. When Caroline tried to persuade her to eat, all she would have was some tea.

'Don't worry about me,' she laid in a low voice, thickened by tears. 'I'll get something for myself when I feel like it.'

'You've had nothing all day,' Caroline said.

'It doesn't matter.' Fenella shut her eyes and turned her face away from Caroline on the pillow, as if she were impatient for her to go.

Caroline hesitated, then sat down on the chair by the bed.

'Fenella, can you listen to me for a moment?' she asked.

'Why?' Fenella said. 'You can't help me.

Nobody can. I've got to go through this by myself.'

Caroline reached for her hand. 'Listen,' she said, 'I want to ask you something. I don't know if it's something important, but it might be.'

Fenella jerked her hand away and flung her arm across her face, almost hiding it. 'I wish you'd leave me.'

'In a moment,' Caroline said. 'Just tell me first, did you mend the reading-lamp that's supposed to have started the fire?'

There was no answer, but she saw Fenella's body stiffen slightly.

'Mrs. Dewhurst told me she saw you doing it,' Caroline went on. 'She may have told the police about it. I thought you ought to know.'

'That damned woman!' Fenella muttered from behind her concealing arm.

'Is it true? Did you do it?' Caroline asked.

There was a pause, then Fenella said, 'I seem to have been answering questions all day, did I this, did I that? And none of it matters, none of it means anything.'

'Did the police ask you anything about that?'

'No, they didn't.'

'But is it true?'

'Yes, it is.'

'You replaced the old flex with a new one only a few days ago?'

'Yes.'

201

'Why didn't you say so then?'

'I don't know. Harry said don't. He said we didn't want a lot of fuss, with the police here, listening to Emma's yarn about the man she heard. He said it would be easiest to stick to the story of the lamp.'

'Do you think he really didn't believe in that man, Fenella, or had he some queer reason for pretending he didn't?'

'Oh God, I don't know!' Fenella's chin began to tremble. 'I never knew what he was thinking. But I did wonder if perhaps he'd started the fire himself.'

'But he'd never do that!' Caroline exclaimed. 'He loved the house.'

'Yes, but at the back of his mind, you know, he wanted to go back to journalism. At least, I often thought so. Only just to pack up and go would have been such a confession of failure. That would have weighed more with him than the insurance. And he was so keen for us all to go out that evening. All the same, I don't think he'd have left Emma in the house to be burnt to death. He wouldn't, would he, Caroline?'

'I'm sure he wouldn't! Think how he rushed in to save her.'

'Yes, and anyway, I was all wrong, because she *must* have heard someone in the house that night. And Harry must have been telling the truth when he said he had enemies who wanted to murder him.'

'But I wonder why he wouldn't let you tell

the police about the lamp.'

'I told you, he didn't want a lot of fuss.'

'It looks almost as if he didn't want Mrs. Dewhurst to tell them about the man.'

'Perhaps, I don't know.' Fenella gave a long sigh. 'None of it matters now.'

'If I were you, though, I'd tell them about the lamp before Mrs. Dewhurst does it for you.'

'All right,' Fenella answered indifferently, a promise, Caroline recognised, that did not mean much.

She stood up. 'There's just one other thing,' she said. 'Have you got a blue coat, Fenella?'

With a start, Fenella sat up in the bed, staring at her.

'A *blue* coat . . . ?'

'Have you?' Caroline asked.

Fenella thrust a hand through the thick blonde hair that tumbled about her face.

'I have, but why you should want to know about it . . . !'

'Where is it?'

'In the cupboard.' Fenella nodded at a cupboard in a corner of the room. 'I haven't worn it for ages.'

Caroline crossed to the cupboard and opened it. She did not see the coat at once, because it had been hung at the back of the cupboard, out of the way. It was navy blue, a quite different colour from her own or Mrs. Dewhurst's.

Closing the cupboard, she turned, to find that Fenella had lain back again, but was watching her still with puzzled intensity. But as soon as Caroline turned towards her, she threw her arm up over her face again.

'I don't understand and I don't care,' Fenella mumbled. 'Take the damned coat away with you, if you want to.'

Caroline lingered in the doorway. 'I wish you'd let me bring you something to eat.'

'No, thank you.'

'Just a little—'

'No, no, no!'

'Well, call me if you want me. I'll be in my room.'

Caroline went quietly out.

She wished that she had Harry's notebook with her now. She would have liked to read it through carefully from beginning to end. But Mr. Sherwin had telephoned the police about it in the afternoon and Sergeant Rutter had come to fetch it. Caroline had had to tell him where she had found it, but that was all he had wanted to know about it then. No doubt Inspector Ingram would ask her some more questions, he had said, when he had had a chance to study it.

She went to the window, leant on the windowsill and gazed out into the darkness of the mild spring night. The air was very still. She could see clumps of white narcissi in the grass and now and then their fragrance came faintly up to her. After the stale smells of charring and damp, the aftermath of the fire, which she had been breathing all day, the scent was wonderfully sweet. But in the distance Jan Pullen was hammering away. Hammer, hammer, hammer!

She tried to put the noise out of her mind. She wanted to think calmly about Harry. By now she was wishing very intensely that she could believe that there was nothing sinister about his curious scrapbook. She would have been most happy if Hugh Sherwin had managed to convince her that it contained nothing but notes for future stories and that there was no need for her to think ill of the dead. But remembering Fenella saying how hard she had tried to make herself trust Harry, and how failing in this had almost driven her out of her mind, Caroline acknowledged that that was the trouble, you simply couldn't trust him. You could be charmed and amused by him, and for days at a time you could like him warmly, and then suddenly something in him that was cold and hard and shut away from you showed itself, something that seemed to be at the very core of his nature.

She thought again of that first meeting of theirs at the station, when she had felt that there was no real friendliness in him, that he was resentful of her and suspicious of her reason for coming. True, in a day or two he seemed to have decided that he had no cause to fear her, and then he and she had been in the accident together, and since then, whatever he had said or done, whatever Fenella had told her about him, it had always been at the back of Caroline's mind that she owed him her life. If she had not developed quite the hero-worship for him that Emma Dewhurst had since he had pulled her out of the fire, if her eyes had not followed him perpetually about the room, if she had never quite lost her dismay at her sense of something profoundly unbalanced in him, she had still found it almost impossible to think about him with any detachment.

Yet quickness of reaction and an unthinking sort of courage are not always united to the other virtues. A man who has them may come out of a war with a chest covered with decorations, then spend the rest of his life floundering helplessly among the less dramatic problems of everyday life. If Harry had been older, Caroline thought, he would probably have been a wonderful commando, with a good many swift killings in the dark to his credit. Born at least ten years too late, the only killing he had had a chance to do had been with his reckless tongue.

And now that he was dead there was very little hope of discovering what compulsions had driven him to attempt so much of that. There was very little hope that she would ever be able to find out the truth about him, to sort out the real from the malicious fantasy, the good from the bad in his nature. Unless, perhaps, she could find out for herself the truth behind the dark hints that he had loved to drop, the truth about the people concerned . . .

She had made up her mind from the start that there was no truth in Harry's allegation that Hugh Sherwin had burnt his bookshop down for the sake of the insurance. That, she was sure, was fantasy.

It was fantasy too that Mrs. Dewhurst had murdered her husband by giving him arsenic in a cup of cocoa. As Sherwin had pointed out, she could not possibly be Mrs. Belper Dewbury, who, murderess or not, had almost certainly been taken dead from the pond in Yorkshire, and who, if she were alive, would be at least ten years older than Emma Dewhurst. It had apparently been the similarity of the names that had been too much for Harry and made him start his cruel teasing. And he had been able to build up his fiction that she was in hiding and afraid of being seen in Rudbourne on the fact of her nervousness about some trouble with her health, perhaps a bad heart.

It was fantasy too that Jack Dawson had tried to kill him. Dawson was just as Jan Pullen had described him, a man driven half-mad by his wife's desertion and probably seeking his own death, rather than that of anyone else, in his dangerous driving. And he could neither have started the fire, nor tampered with Harry's car, since he had been lying in Rudbourne Infirmary with broken ribs.

There remained Jan Pullen. There remained the problem of what he really did in that shed of his half the night. And that should be easy enough to find out.

Caroline left the window, picked up her blue tweed coat, changed her shoes, opened her door cautiously and went softly downstairs.

CHAPTER FIFTEEN

All the lights were out. Emma Dewhurst and Hugh Sherwin had gone to their rooms already. But the front door was unlocked. With no Harry to attend to the matter, it had been forgotten.

Thinking that it would be unfortunate if someone remembered it while she was gone and locked her out, Caroline took the key away with her, locking the door on the outside as she went. Walking to the gate, she kept on the grass at the side of the drive, so that no one in the house should hear her footsteps, for she had a feeling that if Mr. Sherwin heard her, he would come rushing out to stop her. She walked swiftly, reached the gate and started up the road towards the chalk cutting.

As she went, she soon noticed a curious

thing. Jan Pullen's hammering was growing quieter, not louder. It was as Harry had said, it was some strange echo from the hills that made the sound carry so clearly to the house, and it was possible to go much nearer to the garage and hear nothing at all. Caroline presently reached the point where the sound faded altogether. The darkness around her became very still and her own footfalls began to sound very loud on the rough road. She almost missed the noise of hammering, as if there had been something companionable about it. Listening intently, she wondered curiously how long the silence would last, how soon the noise would be audible again.

She was more than half-way to the garage before she realised that the noise really had stopped, that Jan was no longer hammering. It made her feel as if he knew that she was coming. That was unlikely, yet something or someone had interrupted him, and the realisation of it almost made her turn back. If Jan kept the kind of company that she was half-suspicious that he did, she did not in the least want to push her way into it.

But having come as far as she had, it seemed spiritless to give up, when perhaps he had only paused to rest and to smoke a cigarette. She went on and it was only when she was quite near the garage that she admitted to herself that the swimminess in her head and the tightness in her throat was the nausea of intense fear.

The garage itself was all in darkness, with its 'Closed' notice standing in front of the pumps. There was still no sound of hammering coming from it. But Caroline could hear the hammering of her heart with a horrid clarity as she walked softly to the corner of the garage and crept round it to see if there was a light in the old barn behind. There was, but with the sacking nailed across the window, there was no hope of seeing in.

Without any clear plan in her head, she moved nearer to the door. She was thinking that just possibly, if all was quiet, without any sound of voices inside, she might manage to pluck up her courage and simply try walking in. For no reason that she could have explained, she was not really afraid of Jan Pullen. It was the thought of who might be with him that made her shake at the knees. She reached the door, gave herself a moment in which to steady her breathing, then put her ear close to it.

At once she heard a voice, speaking quietly but distinctly. It was Jan's.

'I don't think I'd say any more, if I were you. You aren't in a state to realise what you're saying. It would have been better if you hadn't come. If anyone knows—'

'No one knows.' The voice that interrupted was Fenella's.

For an instant Caroline did not take in that

it really was. She felt as confused as if some trick were being played on her. Less than an hour ago she had left Fenella lying helpless in bed, refusing food and refusing comfort.

But then she heard Jan say, 'What a fool you are, Fenella!'

'Don't say that kind of thing to me!' Fenella cried. 'It's the kind of thing Harry said. I can't stand any more of it.'

'But listen—'

'It's you who's the fool, Jan. That's what I was telling you. You should have given me more time. You should have waited.'

Caroline's first impulse, when she had heard those voices, had been to go away, to go away as fast as she could, to forget them, to blot everything that she had heard completely out of her mind. But she knew that she had no more hope of being able to do that than of forgetting that Harry was dead. She raised a hand and rapped sharply on the door.

There was a sound of startled movement inside. Then, after a short silence, Jan asked, 'Who's there?'

'Caroline.'

At once Fenella answered in a shrill voice, 'Go away, Caroline. I'm quite all right. You needn't have followed me.'

'I didn't follow you,' Caroline said. 'I came to find something out for myself from Jan.'

'He can't tell you anything. Go away. I've got to manage my own life. I don't want you interfering.'

'You might have thought of that a bit sooner.' Caroline grasped the latch and tried to open the door. It did not yield. 'Let me in,' she said.

Jan's voice, closer to the door, said, 'Just a moment.'

A bolt grated and he opened the door.

Caroline took a few steps into the barn, then stood still, looking round it.

At the far end, Fenella was sitting in a broken-down armchair. Her face was pale and puffy from crying and her reddened eyes were defiant. But it was not Fenella whom Caroline had come to see, or who held her attention. It was the barn itself, the workshop where the stolen cars were kept and made over into cars that could safely be sold. Only there were no cars there, either stolen or of any description.

Yet the place was a workshop, a forge or smithy of some kind. It was full of tools for working metal, heavy hammers, queer-shaped tongs, an oxy-acetylene blowlamp. There were also a great many curiously shaped pieces of metal lying around, some on the ground, as if they had been spoiled and thrown away, some on shelves, some dangling from a beam in the roof. Those on the shelves, for the most part, were more or less recognisable as human or animal forms, while those that hung from the beam, stirring continually in an imperceptible current of air, were graceful little bits of

212

abstraction. And in the centre of the floor was a towering thing of intertwined bars, which at first conveyed nothing at all to Caroline, but which, as she stared at it, began to take on disturbing resemblance to several human figures, locked together in a desperate struggle.

As she stood staring at it, Jan said defensively, 'It isn't finished.'

Caroline began to laugh. She laughed helplessly, painfully.

'Don't you dare laugh!' Fenella cried furiously. 'It's a tremendous thing!'

Controlling herself somehow, Caroline said, 'I wasn't laughing at it. I was laughing at myself for thinking Jan was a car-thief.' She turned to the young man. 'But why such secrecy? It's given rise to some very strange ideas.'

'In you?' he asked.

'In me, for one.'

He was looking at her and she suddenly realised why she had always had the feeling that there was something familiar about his steady, thoughtful gaze. It was not because she had ever seen him before, but because she had noticed that way of looking at things in other artists, people who used their eyes for purposes quite strange to almost everyone else, observing, selecting, memorising, taking what they needed from the world around them.

'In Harry too, of course,' she said.

'But he knew all about this.' Jan glanced at Fenella and gave a slight shake of his head, as if he were warning her not to speak. 'It's true I asked him not to spread the story around.'

'Why not?' Caroline asked. 'It isn't a thing people are usually ashamed of.'

He shrugged his shoulders. 'Well, I'm pretty much a beginner and I suppose I felt that if I was never going to get anywhere, I'd sooner not make too much of a song and dance about it beforehand. I'd a good many rows with my family before I broke away and came down here, and I was told so often that I'd never be any good that I suppose I got over-sensitive. All the same, it wasn't actually a secret. If you'd ever asked me about it, I'd have told you.'

'But Harry said—' She stopped.

'You know what Harry was like,' Fenella said.

Caroline nodded. 'Yes, I know.'

'You see, I'd asked him not to talk about what I was doing here,' Jan explained, 'so he didn't, but he couldn't resist making some sort of a story out of it. A crazy story that he probably never expected you to believe.'

Caroline wrinkled her forehead. There was something that the explanation did not cover, something that still wholly bewildered her. She looked at Fenella. 'Did you know the truth?'

'Of course,' Fenella said.

214

'So when Harry told us at breakfast about the racket in stolen cars that he'd run into when he was a reporter, and when he made out that he believed Jan was involved in something of the same sort, you knew he wasn't serious.'

'Of course I did.'

'Then why did he say it at all? And why did it upset you so when he did?'

'He didn't have to have any reason for the things he said—and it was that that upset me.'

'I thought he was saying it simply to annoy you, because he guessed you were in love with Jan,' said Caroline. 'But if you knew the truth about Jan, and Harry knew that you did, what was the point of it?'

'There didn't have to be any point.' Fenella stood up and walked slowly across the barn towards the door. 'Don't you understand even yet that Harry wasn't sane? He didn't have to have any reason for his actions.'

'He'd a reason for the way he talked that morning,' Caroline said. 'I'm sure he had. If it wasn't just to hurt you, he'd some other reason.'

'He could always make people think so, when he wanted to.'

'But what I can't understand—'

'Nobody understands!' Fenella broke in with a flare of anger. 'They talked about his imagination and his exaggeration and they laughed a bit about it and they didn't think it

215

mattered much. But it mattered to me. Living with it was like walking on the edge of a quicksand. You never knew when what you thought was solid ground was going to give way under your feet, when you were going to be up to your neck and drowning.'

Through the rush of passionate words, Caroline tried to keep on the track of her own thought, the one that related to what Harry had said at the breakfast table about the Brig.

'But he can't always have been like that,' she said. 'If he were, he'd never have kept a job as a crime-reporter for twelve years.'

'Oh, he could distinguish between truth and fiction when he wanted to,' Fenella said.

'Then he wasn't insane.'

'It's true you couldn't have had him certified,' Fenella agreed bitterly. 'I couldn't have divorced him. All I could do was decide whether or not I could stand it . . .' She paused in the doorway and looked back at Jan. 'I couldn't have stood it much longer, Jan. You ought to have seen that. If you'd waited, if you'd given me time, I'd have left him. You didn't have to kill him.'

He went a few steps towards her. Then he turned and came back, going to the strange tangle of metal in the middle of the barn and taking hold with both hands of a thick, straining limb that projected out of the group of wrestling figures. It was as if he needed the support it gave him.

In a low voice he said, 'Harry wasn't mad, Caroline. Unbalanced, difficult, too difficult for Fenella. Trying to live with him, she's been coming apart at the seams. Everything's become unreal to her. But don't forget those two men who came around, asking questions about us all. They weren't inventions of Harry's. She and I saw them ourselves. They're real. And my guess is that they were the people who fixed Harry's car. I know I didn't.' The knuckles of his hand turned white as he gripped the iron tighter. 'She knows it really and she'll sort it out for herself when she's had time to think. I'm not a murderer.'

Without answering, Fenella went out into the darkness.

Caroline would have liked to stay for a moment, to give Jan some comfort, some reassurance, but she could hear Fenella's footsteps going swiftly away up the road, and she thought it was best to follow her. Going out, she called to Fenella to wait for her. But though Fenella must have heard her, she did not pause and she was walking too fast for Caroline to catch up with her.

After a minute or two she gave up the attempt. With a frown on her face and her fists clenched in her pockets, she dawdled along, walking slower and slower, thinking again about Harry's notebook, about Mrs. Dewbury who could not be Mrs. Dewhurst, about the Brig. and his gang, of which Jan Pullen after all had not been a member. And there had been the blonde too, who had so discreetly disappeared, presumably with the money. Enough money to buy a nice old house in Dorset?

Why had she thought of that? Oh God, why had she thought of that?

But once she had thought of it, how could she stop thinking of it and of several other things, for instance, that the blonde, if she had helped in the garage, must have been clever at mechanical things? She must have been quite capable of tampering with the steering of a car, and of repairing a reading-lamp in such a way that it would start a fire to destroy the proofs of her past that her husband was holding over her. That scene at the breakfast table, when Harry had told the story of the racket in stolen cars, what had it been but his way of reminding Fenella that as long as he chose to prevent it, he could stop her leaving him for the man she loved?

Caroline found herself shivering. The mild night air seemed to have turned bitterly cold. She started to hurry again and had a stitch in her side and was panting when she reached the house and came face to face with Fenella on the doorstep.

'The door's locked,' Fenella said fretfully. 'I suppose you did that.'

For a moment Caroline could not remember if she had or not. Then she realised

218

that she was clutching the key in her pocket. Without looking at her sister, she pushed the key into the lock and turned it.

The door would not open.

'Here, let me,' Fenella said impatiently, and tried the handle.

'I think it's bolted,' Caroline said.

'What damned fool's done that?' Fenella demanded. 'We'll have to try the back door.' Muttering at the stupidity of people who did not mind their own business, she set off round the house.

Caroline went after her. But the back door would not open either.

'We'll have to wake someone,' Fenella said.

She went on until she was under Hugh Sherwin's window. There was still a light in it and when Fenella called, he appeared at it immediately.

'Mrs. Lyddon!' he exclaimed, peering down at them in the darkness. 'Miss Dyer! What's happened?'

'Nothing,' Fenella answered. 'We went for a walk and we've been locked out. Do you mind coming down and letting us in?'

'Yes, yes, of course—just wait a minute.' His head disappeared.

Fenella and Caroline returned to the front door. As they passed under Mrs. Dewhurst's window a light came on behind the drawn curtains, but she did not look out. However, when Mr. Sherwin drew back the bolts on the door and opened it, she was at the top of the stairs, clutching her dressing-gown around her, her hair in rollers, her face shiny with skin-food, and her mouth, without any lipstick on it, working as usual, as she gave little gasps and hisses of alarm.

'Sorry to get you up, Mr. Sherwin,' Fenella said, 'but you needn't have bolted the door. Harry and I never bothered to do that.'

Her tone said that she thought a mere paying guest had no right to take such a responsibility upon himself.

'I didn't, as a matter of fact,' he said, 'though I might have, if I'd thought of it. I'd no idea you two had gone out.'

Mrs. Dewhurst came a few steps down the stairs.

'I locked up, dear,' she said. 'I'm so sorry. I thought I heard something, so I got up to listen and I heard the door downstairs close very softly. Of course it must have been when you went out, but I didn't think of that. I just thought of the man who was prowling around on the night of the fire. So when everything was quiet I came down and bolted the door, and made sure the back door was locked too, and checked all the windows. I'm so sorry, dear.'

Caroline thought of Harry asking if she could imagine Emma getting up in the night to investigate a strange noise downstairs. He had said that she would be more likely to pull the bedclothes over her head and start praying. That showed again how wrong he could be. He had been wrong about everyone, about everything. There wasn't a word he had said that you could safely believe.

'You should have called me, Mrs. Dewhurst,' Mr. Sherwin said. 'It can't have been pleasant, prowling about by yourself.'

Harry had mocked the little woman for the same thing, Caroline remembered, calling her wonderful, brave Emma. But it appeared that she had her own sort of bravery.

'I didn't want to disturb poor Fenella,' she said. 'I thought if she'd managed to get to sleep, she oughtn't to be woken up. I know what it is, you see. I know how difficult it is sometimes to sleep, just when you need it most.'

'I couldn't sleep,' Fenella said. 'That's why I went out.'

'That was sensible,' Mrs. Dewhurst said. 'The fresh air sometimes helps. I hope you'll sleep now. Good night.' She turned and went back to her room.

Fenella hesitated, then began to climb the stairs after her.

Caroline stood watching her, thinking, 'Not now—I couldn't bear to say anything now. With those drooping shoulders, and that thin trailing hand on the banisters, and her hair all over the place, she looks just as she used to when she came back from a day at school that

221

she'd hated more than usual. How she hated it at school. And how she hated the holidays. How she's hated almost everything. Poor Fenella . . .'

Behind Caroline, Mr. Sherwin had been locking and bolting the door again. Then, considerably to her surprise, because it seemed unlike one of his gestures, he put an arm round her shoulders and drew her towards the bottom of the stairs.

'I know you won't listen to me if I ask you again to go back to London tomorrow,' he said, 'but will you at least go to bed and have a good rest? I don't think there's anything you can do for your sister just now.'

She looked at him quickly, wondering if she had heard something more in his voice than there was in the mere words.

At that moment the doorbell rang.

They looked at one another. Neither of them moved. The bell rang again and was followed by the clatter of the knocker.

Mr. Sherwin looked at his watch. It was as if he felt that finding out what the time was would tell them something about whoever was at the door.

'Eleven-fifteen,' he muttered. 'Late for callers.'

'Unless perhaps it's the police.' Caroline was very tense and as she watched him go to the door she would have liked to bolt up the stairs after Fenella.

When he opened the door, a small man with thin, foxy features and a crooked smile that revealed discoloured teeth stepped forward quickly and planted a foot inside the house. Standing close behind him was a much bigger man, with a paunch that bulged over his belt and a loose grin that showed false teeth of a dazzling whiteness. Caroline could not see if he had hands like hams and a broken little finger, because he kept both hands hidden in his pockets.

'It's all right, we aren't here to make trouble,' the small man said, beaming on her and Hugh Sherwin with a dreadful friendliness. 'No need to get upset, mister. All we want's the blonde.'

CHAPTER SIXTEEN

'I think there's some mistake,' Mr. Sherwin replied calmly.

'Look,' the small man said, 'didn't I say we don't want trouble? But we've got to talk to the blonde. We know she's here. I've seen her once already.'

'I'm sorry, Mrs. Lyddon can't possibly see you tonight,' Mr. Sherwin answered.

'Lyddon—that's what she is these days, is it?' The small man laughed. 'Well, she can see us all right. You go and ask her.'

'And tell her we don't want trouble,' said the big man behind him. 'She needn't be afraid. All we want's our rights.'

'That's right,' said the small man. 'Our share, that's all. We're reasonable.'

Hugh Sherwin went a step closer to them. At the same time his hand, behind him, where they could not see it, started to signal something to Caroline.

At first she did not understand, then she realised that he was pointing towards the room where the telephone was. Call the police, his jabbing finger was saying.

To the two men, he repeated, 'Mrs. Lyddon can't possibly see you. You'd better go.'

'Now, now,' the small man said, 'no need to get nasty, is there? I told you, we don't mean any harm. Calling so late, it looks bad, I know, but we've come a long way, that's all, couldn't get here sooner. We don't aim to touch a hair of her head—or yours either, if you go and get her.'

One would have had to be deaf not to hear the menace in his voice. It was why Caroline took no notice of that signalling finger. If she moved, she thought, it would only precipitate trouble. The trouble was coming anyhow and delaying it might not help, but could hardly make matters worse.

With his thin, stooping figure still blocking the doorway, Mr. Sherwin said, 'You're taking a big risk, coming back. Don't you know the police are looking for you for Lyddon's murder?'

'*Murder?*' the little man cried shrilly, almost as if it were a word that he had never heard before, and looking as if hearing it now had given him a very unpleasant shock, had jarred him badly. 'You said *murder?*'

'Yes, of Harry Lyddon,' Mr. Sherwin replied evenly. 'And the police are looking for the two men who've been in this neighbourhood recently, asking questions about the people in this house—two men who've been identified as members of a gang of car-thieves.'

In the midst of her fear for them all and of the confusion in her mind about Fenella, Caroline thrilled with admiration at the calm with which he continued to speak. His tone expressed only the reserved disapproval with which, no doubt, he would have got rid of an unwelcome customer who had come to his bookshop in search of obscene publications.

'Now wait a minute, mister!' The small man put a hand on Mr. Sherwin's chest, pushed him backwards and stepped into the house. 'Now wait a minute! Don't you go getting any wrong ideas into your head about Jim and me. If there's been a murder, it had nothing to do with us . . . All right, lady!' He rapped the words out sharply, turning his yellow-toothed grin on Caroline. 'I can see you teetering there, trying to make up your mind to run for the phone. Don't you try it, not while my friend and me are here. Now—' He turned back to Mr. Sherwin. 'What happened?'

'I told you, Harry Lyddon was killed this morning,' the bookseller answered.

'Murdered?'

'Yes.'

'How?'

'I understand that someone tampered with the steering of his new car. He lost control of it on the hill and it crashed into the wall of the garage at the bottom.'

A shudder shook the small man's skinny body. 'Jim, did you hear that? Someone tampered with the poor devil's steering.'

'That's right,' the big man said stolidly. One of his hands came out of his pocket to grasp the other man's shoulder and push him forward. 'Let's get a move on and get out.'

'Murder, he said!' The small man's teeth were chattering. 'We never put our hands to murder. When did it happen, this murder?'

The big man said, 'This morning is what he said. So get a move on, Bill. We've nothing to worry about, but the sooner we're through here the better.'

'I said Lyddon was killed this morning,' Mr. Sherwin said. 'But the tampering with the car, naturally, was done earlier.'

'How much earlier?' the little man asked quickly.

'It could have been any time after the car was last used,' Mr. Sherwin said. 'That was

226

about five o'clock yesterday afternoon.'

'There! You're right, Jim, nothing to worry about at all.' Another wide grin split across the small man's face and some colour came back into it. He turned to Caroline, as if he wanted her to share in his good news. 'Five o'clock yesterday to past five o'clock today Jim and me were in London. We can prove it easy. Got a dozen people who'll prove it. Come along in, Jim. We'd better get what we came for.'

Mr. Sherwin made one more heroic try. 'Only you're too late, I'm afraid. The police have got it already.'

Jim put one of his huge hands on the small man's shoulder again, pushed him to one side and faced Mr. Sherwin himself. 'And left her around loose—no, mister, that's one thing they wouldn't do. Now we're coming in and if you don't give us trouble, we won't give you trouble, but God help you if you try to get in the way.'

His other hand came out of his pocket. There was a gun in it.

Caroline screamed. Then she realised that someone else was screaming, was going on and on screaming and the shocking thing was that it was Jim himself. And there had been a loud bang, as if a gun had been fired, yet he had not even started to raise it. Instead, he had let it slip out of his hand to the floor, while his arm dangled limply above it, with a streak of red running out from under his sleeve and forming

227

in a great drop on the end of one of his fingers.

His screams changed to curses as both Bill and Mr. Sherwin dived for the gun on the floor together.

'Leave it—come on, we're getting out of here!' Jim bellowed and turned and staggered out of the door.

As he went there was another bang. A starry circle of splinters formed on the door-frame. This time Caroline saw the gun from which it had come. It was pointing through the bannisters at the top of the stairs and wavering about in a most terrifying manner.

Crouching behind the bannisters, still in her dressing-gown, with the rollers in her hair and the skin-food glistening on her colourless face, was Emma Dewhurst. From where Caroline stood, it looked as if her eyes were tight shut, but as if, nevertheless, she was nerving herself to pull the trigger again. Near her, pale as a ghost, yet with an expression of deep indifference on her face, stood Fenella.

'Don't!' Caroline shouted. 'Don't, Emma—you've done enough!'

Mrs. Dewhurst did not hear her. Another bullet spat, this time through the open door into the darkness.

Abandoning the gun on the floor, the small man sprang away from Mr. Sherwin and made for the door. Mr. Sherwin slammed it behind him. Caroline dashed to the telephone.

While she was speaking to someone in the

police-station, she heard Mr. Sherwin say, 'Nice shooting, Emma.'

Her answer was a wail of terror. 'Have they gone, Mr. Sherwin? Are you sure they've gone?'

'Gone and I shouldn't think they'll be coming back,' he said as he picked up the gun on the floor and looked at it thoughtfully.

'That awful man!' she gasped. 'I thought he was going to kill you and then all the rest of us. But I didn't mean to hit him. I thought I'd just shoot over their heads and frighten them. I didn't mean to hit him, Mr. Sherwin. Do you think the police will believe that?'

'Whatever they believe, you've several grateful witnesses that it was self-defence,' he said.

Mrs. Dewhurst gave another wail. 'I feel awful—awful! I never meant to hit him. I know if I'd tried to, I'd never have hit him at all.'

'Well, come down and have a drink,' Sherwin said. 'That's what we all need.'

'A cup of tea,' she said. 'That's what I'd like.'

She started down the staircase, one hand clutching her dressing-gown around her, the other holding the gun.

At the bottom Mr. Sherwin waited, also gun in hand.

Fenella, still motionless on the landing above, suddenly began to giggle hysterically.

'Look at them!' she screamed. 'Look at

them! When are they going to start shooting it out? Which of them is faster on the draw?'

Mr. Sherwin gave a start, as if he had only just realised what he was holding.

'I think I'd put my money on Mrs. Dewhurst,' he said. 'It's a long time since I've had to use one of these things.'

'It's the first time I've ever used mine,' Mrs. Dewhurst said, 'I mean, since my dear husband taught me how. And even then, I hated it. But he said I ought to be able to, because of the times when he had to go away and I was alone in the house. There was sometimes a lot of money in the till and he was always afraid we'd be robbed.'

'Fenella,' Caroline said, returning from the telephone, 'don't you think you ought to go back to bed now? The police will be here soon, and you don't want to have to talk to them again, do you?'

As she spoke, she saw Mr. Sherwin give her a quick glance, but she pretended not to have seen it. Her suggestion, however, as usual, had a contrary effect on Fenella. Still smiling and making queer little muffled sounds that might have been giggles or sobs, she came down the stairs.

'I'm sorry,' she tittered. 'I know I'm being silly, but I can't help it. It's Emma—Emma and her gun. I've never seen anything so funny. To think she's had it hidden away somewhere all this time. Here in our house. How Harry would have loved that if he'd known. Can't you imagine what he'd have made of it?'

Her laughter began to get out of control. She clung to Caroline to steady herself.

'It—it just shows how wrong he was about people, doesn't it?' she sobbed on to Caroline's shoulder. 'He always used to say Emma poisoned her husband with a cup of cocoa, but she'd never have done that when she had such a nice little gun, would she?'

Mrs. Dewhurst patted her arm.

'What you really need, dear, is something to eat,' she said kindly. 'I know you've had nothing all day. Come into the kitchen. I'll warm you up a nice cup of soup.'

Fenella let herself be led into the kitchen. Caroline and Mr. Sherwin followed.

Filling the electric kettle, Caroline plugged it in and started to make tea, while Mrs. Dewhurst, with her gun making a bulge in the pocket of her dressing-gown, opened a can of chicken soup and began to warm it up. Mr. Sherwin remained in the doorway, thoughtfully watching the three women.

There was something very tense about him, as if he were waiting for something. The police, Caroline thought. How much he might have guessed earlier she did not know, but he had had time since the visit of the two men to put two and two together. He knew that they had come for Fenella. He knew that they were members of the gang of car-thieves. He did

231

not need to know the other things that Caroline knew.

Fenella had sat down at the table and put her elbows on it. She held her long white face between her hands. She could not stop talking.

'I don't understand about those men,' she said. 'What they wanted. But I haven't been thinking clearly about anything all day. I've only been thinking about Harry—and Jan, of course. D'you know, I felt sure straight away it was Jan who killed Harry and that it was all my fault. I couldn't think about anything else. I completely forgot those men and the man Emma saw on the night of the fire. Harry said there wasn't a man. He said Emma'd never really have dared to get up to investigate if she'd heard someone. But he was wrong there too. Emma's very brave.'

'Oh, my dear, I'm not,' Mrs. Dewhurst said, stirring the soup. 'I was shaking like a jelly.'

'Of course, you had your gun,' Fenella went on. 'Harry didn't know about that. Did you have your gun with you that night, Emma?'

'Well yes, as a matter of fact, I did,' Mrs. Dewhurst said, 'and of course it helped.'

'And tonight too, when you came down and locked up?'

'Yes, but Harry was quite right about me, I'm not brave, not at all. He'd know that, because he was so brave himself.'

'Those men, though—what did they want? And what had they got against Harry? Had he really some information about them? Because they did kill him, didn't they?' Fenella looked up questioningly at Mr. Sherwin.

He avoided her gaze, frowning down at the gun in his hand. He replied haltingly, 'They told us they'd an alibi, Mrs. Lyddon. They said they could prove they were in London.'

The kettle was boiling. Caroline poured the water into the teapot.

'I suppose alibis can be fixed,' she said.

'But I don't think they even knew about the murder,' he said. 'I had an impression that it was a real shock when they heard it.'

Caroline, who had had the same impression, stayed silent, but Mrs. Dewhurst, who was cutting some bread to make toast to go with the soup for Fenella, said positively, 'Well, I don't agree, Mr. Sherwin. I think that was just put on, and I'll tell you why. That big man, the awful man I shot, was the one I saw on the night of the fire . . . Oh yes.' She nodded earnestly as she trimmed the crusts off the bread. 'I couldn't remember him before, but I knew him at once when I saw him again.'

'What a pity you didn't shoot him the first time,' Fenella said with a heavy sigh. 'Are you sure it was the same man? Can you swear to it when the police ask you?'

'Well, I—I suppose so, dear.' Mrs. Dewhurst did not sound quite so certain any more. 'I'll certainly tell them that I think so.'

'Then you *aren't* quite sure,' Fenella

233

persisted.

As Mrs. Dewhurst hesitated, Mr. Sherwin said, 'I think Mrs. Dewhurst is wise not to be too definite. The men, after all, may have another alibi for the night of the fire. Besides, it's a rather strange thing she's told us.'

'Strange?' she said. 'You mean that I recognised him when I couldn't remember him before?'

'No, that's quite a common phenomenon, after something like a blow on the head,' he said. 'I meant strange that you remember him at all, because I could have sworn, with all respect, that Lyddon was right when he said there wasn't any man in the house that night—except, of course, Lyddon himself.'

'I'm sorry, I don't understand,' Mrs. Dewhurst said. 'Of course Harry was there.' She gave a bewildered frown. 'But that was afterwards, when he rescued me. It was the other man I heard downstairs, before the fire started.'

'Then what happened to your gun?'

The soup chose that moment to boil over. Mrs. Dewhurst snatched it up from the stove.

'Why, I—I don't remember,' she said. 'Isn't that odd? I suppose I dropped it.'

'Then who picked it up?'

'I don't know. Perhaps Harry did.'

'And gave it back to you?'

She shook her head. 'I—I don't think so. I think he must just have put it back in my drawer. I haven't given it a thought till this moment.'

'He put it back in your drawer and never said anything about it to you or anyone else?' Mr. Sherwin said.

Caroline, who had been pouring out the tea, caught the change in his voice and turned to look at him. There was a look of great strain on his face and his eyes were feverishly bright.

'Yes, isn't it odd?' Mrs. Dewhurst repeated. 'I ought to have thought about it. But I'm so muddled about everything that happened that night.'

'I think perhaps it's just a little too odd,' Mr. Sherwin said quietly. 'If you'd had your gun with you that night and Lyddon had found it, he'd never have given it back to you. You had him far too scared by then.'

'Scared?' she said incredulously. 'Harry scared—of *me*?'

'Why not? Speaking for myself, I find you a quite terrifying woman.' As he spoke, he shifted his position slightly and Caroline saw that the gun in his hand was no longer pointing at the floor. He had lifted it a little to point it at the plump, soft-looking little woman by the stove. 'Only Lyddon didn't realise that till after the fire, did he? Or perhaps he wouldn't have troubled to rescue you. It's puzzling in a way why he did. Was it a momentary real generosity of spirit, or couldn't he bear to lose his source of income? A blackmailer, after all, has the best of reasons to be concerned for the safety of his victim.'

Fenella drew her breath in sharply. 'Blackmail! Then that *was* how he got it, all that money . . .' She looked up at Caroline. 'It *was*, I wasn't mad.'

Caroline's hand dropped on to Fenella's shoulder and Fenella clung to it.

'Mr. Sherwin, you said blackmail . . .' she said.

'I'm afraid so, Mrs. Lyddon,' he replied. 'I don't know how much it was, and whether he needed the money, or just the pleasant feeling of power. Unfortunately he didn't realise the kind of person he was dealing with. He never dreamt Mrs. Dewhurst had it in her to hit back.'

'Hit back at Harry?' Mrs. Dewhurst said with a little sob. 'When he'd saved my life? Why, I'd have done anything for him—anything.'

Mr. Sherwin nodded. 'It was when you started that line with Lyddon that he got frightened. It was in here, I remember. You took his hand as if you were going to kiss it in your tremendous gratitude and he snatched it away from you as if you were a snake that was trying to bite him. Because, after all, he knew you'd started the fire yourself to destroy his records, and he knew he was the man who'd knocked you out, before he decided to save you, and he knew you knew that. So that display of gratitude warned him what you had in you, and from then on he became very quiet and subdued and tried to deny knowing anything important about anybody. And if he'd found you'd a gun, he'd never have given it back to you.'

Caroline could not keep quiet any longer. 'Do you mean she did poison her husband? Is she Mrs. Dewbury?'

'I don't think she's either Mrs. Dewbury or Mrs. Dewhurst,' he answered. 'That was just one of Lyddon's twisted jokes, very typical of him. Inducing her, I mean, when he helped to hide her here, to call herself by that name, because every time he used it, and let her know what he was saying about her, she'd be reminded of what he could say about her if he chose, which was that she was the disappearing blonde, who helped the Brig. in his garage, the one who got away with the money when he went to prison and whom the gang have only just tracked down. A skilled mechanic, naturally, who'd know just how to tamper with the steering of a car . . . *No, don't do that!*' He rapped the words out sharply as Mrs. Dewhurst's hand started scrabbling to get inside the pocket of her dressing-gown, where she had put her gun. The gun in his own hand was quite steady. If it was a long time since he had had to use one, it was plain that once he had known very well what to do with one when he must.

'Mrs. Lyddon, you're nearest,' he said. 'Do you think you can take that thing away from her? But be careful not to get between her and me.'

Emma Dewhurst gave a tremulous little sigh. With woeful eyes, which had begun to mist with tears in their familiar way, she watched as Fenella stood up, came towards her and reached hesitantly for the gun.

Then she threw the saucepanful of hot soup straight in Fenella's face.

CHAPTER SEVENTEEN

Fenella gave a cry and flung her arms up. In that instant Emma Dewhurst slipped behind her. The gun came out of her pocket.

'Drop that gun, Mr. Sherwin,' she ordered as she dug the barrel into Fenella's ribs, 'or I'll let her have it.'

Her plump face was as impassive as ever, except for the wriggling of the lips that issued the improbable words.

Reluctantly Hugh Sherwin laid the gun down on the kitchen table.

'What's the point of this?' he asked. 'You can't get away. The police will be here at any moment.'

'You never know what you can do till you try,' Mrs. Dewhurst answered. 'No, dear!' she added sharply, as she saw Caroline make a movement towards Fenella. 'Don't come any nearer. You've been very good to me, I'm quite fond of you and I don't want to hurt you. You've all been good to me and I was very happy here till Harry started playing his games with me. I didn't even mind that much as long as he was just asking me for money. I'm like that, you know. Anyone can get round me if they get on the right side of me. But when he got that ridiculous idea in his head that that drunk who knocked him off the road had done it on purpose because I'd told him to, and when he started threatening me in front of you all, that was really too much. I didn't like it any more. I warned him. You all heard me. I said, "You're a very foolish young man," I said, "it's a terrible thing to have an enemy".'

She was edging her way forward until she could reach the gun on the table. Fenella stood paralysed, afraid to look round at her, afraid to make any movement to wipe the scalding soup from her face.

'It's all such a pity,' Mrs. Dewhurst went on with one of her woebegone sighs. 'I was quite happy here and really quite truly grateful to poor Harry for giving me such a nice home and looking after me so well. He promised me he would. "You'll see, I'm a wonderful cook," he said, that time he recognised me in Newcastle and said if I'd give him fifteen hundred pounds he could put down the deposit on a lovely house he'd heard about and give me a place to stay until Brigadier Lemarnier came out of gaol. And it was quite true, he was a wonderful cook, and I didn't grudge him the money he used to ask for from time to time. I knew he didn't waste it, he just used it to make things nicer for us all. But then when Jim and Bill traced me and he had the accident which had nothing to do with them or me at all, he seemed to lose his head. I said to him, "Harry dear," I said, "I must go away for a time now, because those wretched men won't be reasonable, they'll rob me of all I have, and then where will you be?" And he thought I meant to disappear and not help him any more, and he wouldn't listen to me when I said I'd be sure to let him know where I'd gone. As if I'd even thought of disappearing! I needed him, you know, as much as he needed me. So it's all a great pity. Now, Caroline dear . . .' She moved away from Fenella towards Caroline. 'You'll come with me, won't you? I've a few things upstairs I shouldn't like to leave behind. And I shouldn't try coming after us, Mr. Sherwin, or getting out of the window, or anything like that, because I'll have Caroline with me.'

With a small gesture, she indicated that Mr. Sherwin was to get out of the way.

He hesitated, then as he moved away from the doorway, his eyes met Caroline's. They seemed to be trying to tell her something, but she did not understand what it was, except that it was meant somehow to reassure her.

Mrs. Dewhurst smiled as if she wanted to reassure Caroline too and nodded to her to go out of the room ahead of her.

Caroline went a few steps, was aware of swift movement behind her and realised what Mr. Sherwin's glance had been trying to tell her. Inspector Ingram and Sergeant Rutter were on either side of the door. As Emma Dewhurst went through it, the inspector's hand came down powerfully on her wrist. The gun went off, but like the earlier shot that she had fired from it, buried itself harmlessly in the doorpost.

Later Mr. Sherwin told Caroline that the police had been there for some minutes. He had left the door ajar for them when the three women had gone ahead of him into the kitchen after Mrs. Dewhurst's rout of Bill and Jim, then he had stayed in the kitchen doorway, where he could signal to Ingram and Rutter when they arrived. It had been only after they had come that he had started to question Mrs. Dewhurst about the man whom she had said that she had seen in the house on the night of the fire.

'I thought I'd arranged everything so neatly,' Mr. Sherwin said, 'and I never even thought of watching that pot of soup. I'm afraid I'm not cut out for the tough stuff.' He and Caroline were in the basement of the bookshop in Rudbourne. 'This sort of thing suits me much better.'

'Me too.' The basement felt such a safe and restful place to be that Caroline hardly noticed the smell of mould, or minded the thick dust on the books.

She was helping Mr. Sherwin to sort them. Her part of the job, the wholly unskilled part, was to pick them up one at a time, rub the dust off them and hand them on to him. He glanced at them and dumped them on various piles. It was soothing work, as he had promised that it would be, good occupational therapy for a convalescent, if, he had said, she wanted, just for a change, to behave like one.

At the back of her mind Caroline was aware that she would have found almost anything good occupational therapy just then so long as she was doing it with him, but she did not dream of saying so. He was not a man to whom it would ever feel easy to say anything like that, or not until you knew him really well. And that would take how long? A year? A lifetime? Perhaps that depended on you, and whether or not you were ready to push up your sleeves for the job and go in fighting.

'I still keep thinking about Harry,' she said, 'and trying to understand all those pointless lies he told. What was his real reason for pretending he thought Jan Pullen was mixed up with the car-thieves, when he knew he wasn't, and that you set this place on fire?'

Mr. Sherwin frowned at the battered book in his hand and tossed it on to the pile of worthless volumes.

'Wasn't it a sort of smoke-screen?' he said. 'The lies weren't pointless.'

Caroline reached for another book and blew the thick coating of dust off it.

'A smoke-screen?'

'Well, he'd got on to something real, hadn't he? He'd recognised Emma Dewhurst as the blonde who'd been involved in Brigadier Lemarnier's racket. He'd got the money out of her to buy the house he yearned for, and he was getting more money out of her whenever he felt like it. And at the same time he was having his own peculiar sort of fun with her, one day frightening her to death that he was going to give her away, and the next day charming her so and feeding her so well that she felt happy and safe again and didn't want to move away. But being Harry, he couldn't keep quiet about it. To enjoy the game to the full, he had to talk about it. Yet he couldn't tell the truth, even to his wife, or it would have spoilt everything, so he muddled it all up a bit, and Mrs. Dewhurst became a murderess. But in case that drew too much attention to her, the rest of us came in for some of the same sort of thing. I became an arsonist and Pullen a car-thief. And naturally by the time he'd spread all those stories around, no one was taking him seriously. But Mrs. Dewhurst always knew what he meant—that he was reminding her of his power over her.'

'He must have wished he hadn't talked quite so much about how easy it was to get away with arson,' Caroline said, 'because I should think that it was that that gave her the idea of burning his desk and files when she hadn't been able to break into them.' She began to turn the pages of the book that she was holding. It was an old book, with a worn binding and discoloured pages. 'It's funny how one automatically thinks of a blonde as fairly young. At least, I did when I read about her in Harry's notebook. Yet if Emma bleached her hair as drastically as she's been dyeing it black, people would call her a blonde, whatever age she was, even if there was a sort of mockery in the way they said it. As it was, I thought—I actually thought that Fenella . . .' Her voice quavered. To steady herself, she stared hard at the book in her hands. It had some rather attractive illustrations, she realised, line-drawings of insects and plant cells.

After a moment, Mr. Sherwin said, 'I know what you thought. I saw it in your face when we were all in the kitchen and you were trying to make your sister go upstairs before the police arrived, so that you could warn her.'

'But I thought you thought the same yourself,' she said. 'When those men asked for the blonde, you answered as if you thought they meant Fenella. You said Mrs. Lyddon couldn't see them.'

'Because I knew Mrs. Dewhurst was on the landing with a gun and I didn't want her to take it into her head to start shooting us all, because we knew who she was.' He gave his dry laugh. 'Actually I suspected your sister of something quite different. For a time I was fairly sure she'd set fire to the house, to force her husband to give it up and go back to the sort of life she preferred. And I thought he knew that and that when he started being so positive that the fire had been caused by a mere fault in the wiring, and discouraging drama of all kinds, he was trying to protect her.'

'Mrs. Dewhurst wanted us to think Fenella started the fire,' Caroline said. 'She told me about seeing her mending the reading-lamp. She also told me Fenella had a blue coat. That was to cover up the mistakes she made when she asked me if I was wearing my blue coat when the van ran into Harry's car. She was afraid then that that wasn't an accident and that Bill and Jim had been after her.'

'And Lyddon was afraid they'd been after him.'

'Yet at first he didn't seem to believe in them. He didn't seem to believe Fenella or Jan when they told him about them.'

'Don't you think he was just doing his best not to believe in them, because he was really very badly scared? He scared quite easily, once he had time to think. It was only when he didn't give himself time to start imagining things that he was really courageous.'

'As he was when he dashed into the fire to save that awful woman.'

'Or to save his house, or his source of income. We'll never quite know what his motive was. Anyway, he wasn't a murderer, whatever else was wrong with him, so when he'd knocked her out in sheer fury, just as she was probably going to come rushing out screaming to meet us, he didn't leave her to burn, but brought her out.'

'I remember he stayed near her until she recovered consciousness,' Caroline said. 'I suppose he was waiting to hear what story she was going to tell. I listened to them both, but I didn't suspect anything.' She looked up at him. 'When did you first start to suspect her?'

'When you showed me the notebook. Dewhurst—Dewbury—the names were too much of a coincidence. It struck me it meant there was some connection between her and Lyddon that we didn't know about and that he'd chosen the name for her. Yet she couldn't be Mrs. Dewbury. Then I realised that she could be the blonde, and as soon as I thought of that, everything began to fit.'

'I wish I'd thought of it too, instead of the nonsense I did think . . . Mr. Sherwin, I don't know what this book is, but it's nice. If the price isn't right out of my reach, I'd like to buy it.'

'I'll make you a present of it.' Smiling, he held out his hand for it.

Then his face changed. Pushing his spectacles up on to his forehead, he started to turn the pages, holding them close to his naked eyes.

'I'm afraid it's not in good condition,' he said, 'but if you'd like it . . .' With the warmest smile that Caroline had seen him give, he held it out to her.

'But what is it?' she asked.

'Hooke's *Micrographia.*'

'Oh, but that's something fearfully valuable, isn't it? I can't possibly take it.'

'It's not as valuable as I'd like it to be. I doubt if it's worth much more than two hundred.'

'Two hundred *pounds*?' she said.

He was still holding it out. 'I'd like you to have it.'

She shook her head. 'But perhaps it's a start, an omen. You said that if you found only a few worthwhile things in this junk, it might give you some heart to go on. So let's look for some more.'

'Take it,' he said. 'Please. I should feel so— so extraordinarily happy if it turned out that you could develop an interest in old books.'

They looked at each other for a moment, then Caroline reached out her hands for it.

We hope you have enjoyed this Large Print book. Other Chivers Press or G.K. Hall & Co. Large Print books are available at your library or directly from the publishers.

For more information about current and forthcoming titles, please call or write, without obligation, to:

Chivers Press Limited
Windsor Bridge Road
Bath BA2 3AX
England
Tel. (01225) 335336

OR

G.K. Hall & Co.
295 Kennedy Memorial Drive
Waterville
Maine 04901
USA

All our Large Print titles are designed for easy reading, and all our books are made to last.